Janie
TSE-NI (JAY NEE)
OF CHEROKEE

Third Book in the Trilogy of "White Feather"

By

Nancy McIntosh Pafford

Nancy m Pafford

Catch the Spirit of Appalachia, Inc.
WESTERN NORTH CAROLINA

FIRST PRINTING

Other Books by the Author:
White Feather
Cherokee Rose
Oscar, the Legendary Alligator

Note to the Reader: The story White Feather, Cherokee Rose and Janie and other characters are fictional; however, the events in the story are based on factual research accounts of the history of the Cherokee people.

Layout by Amy Ammons Garza
Cover Illustration by Doreyl Ammons Cain

Published by
SAN NO. 8 5 1 – 0 8 8 1
Catch the Spirit of Appalachia, Inc.
29 Regal Avenue, Sylva, NC 28779
Phone: 828-631-4587

Library of Congress Control Number: 2010937956

ISBN: 978-0-9827611-5-1

This book is

DEDICATED

TO THE

CHEROKEE CHILDREN

When I enter your school campus
I see this sign:

"Committed to —
Empowering our students
Preserving our nation
Ensuring our future"

Remember you are the future!

Be Strong!

—Nancy McIntosh Pafford

Thank You!

...Zellna Shaw for your continued interest in this story...proofreading my manuscript and making helpful suggestions. I appreciate all you have done, so...
THIS BOOK IS FOR YOU, MY FRIEND!

...Jerry Wolf, distinguished Cherokee elder, for sharing wonderful Cherokee stories, taking me to stickball games and to the Cherokee weddings you have conducted. I appreciate your patiently answering my many questions concerning the history, culture and lifestyles of the Cherokee people.
Gv-ge-yu

...The Ammons Sisters, two very talented ladies—Amy, my editor, and Doreyl, my artist. I am grateful for your help. It's been a wonderful privilege and honor working with you again.

...Karen Royce. Sharing your knowledge about wolves and patiently answering my many questions about their habits is greatly appreciated.

...David Smith at Bearmeat's Indian Den. I appreciate your friendship and interest in my books, and encouraging me to get this book completed! Thank you for opening your beautiful shop to me for many book signings.

...Tim, my son, for encouraging me to write...and for having a birthmark of a little red arrowhead on your back.

...Cherokee friends who answered questions during interviews with them while I was writing this book.

Prologue 1995

It was a beautiful clear day in early spring with many colors glowing on the mountain sides as Janie and Russ traveled along the winding road.

This was Janie's favorite time of year when the rodedemdrum, roses and all the other wild flowers painted their own panoramic canvases. Days like today made Janie want to paint every scene as it appeared along the highway. Her love for art was shared by her husband and he encouraged her with his support. They led busy lives and this drive gave them the opportunity to relax and share their new joy.

"Grandmother Rose will be thrilled when we tell her our news," Janie laughed softly, turning to look at her husband driving the car. "I'm glad we waited to tell her in person instead of calling on the phone."

Russ nodded, then glanced at Janie and smiled.

"I can't wait to see her face when we tell her that she is going to be a great grandmother," Janie said, patting the little bulge in her stomach.

The couple had been married for two years...two years of complete happiness...and now more joy was headed their way. They had planned to visit Rose sooner, but the Native American Art Gallery they owned kept them busy and they had not been able to leave the store. They were delighted when Hunter and Emily, Janie's brother and sister, offered to manage the shop for a few days so the couple could finally visit Rose.

Shifting her weight Janie sighed.

"Are you getting tired?" Russ asked.

"A little," she answered.

"We can stop and rest for a while if you like," offered Russ.

"No, don't stop. I'll be fine." Janie reached over and caressed his shoulder knowing that he was also tired from the long drive. "We'll be there soon. We're about fifty miles from Grandmother's home."

Russ nodded.

They rode on in silence, enjoying the beauty of the tall mountains on each side of the road.

The late afternoon sun had streaked them in many shades of green and a new scene appeared at each turn in the highway as they followed the meandering river. The sun would soon drop behind the tall sloping peaks, but now its rays cast dark shadows on the ridges and valleys, turning them into a smoky blue.

"Russ, I'm anxious for you to see grandmother's cabin. My Grandfather Hunter, oops, forgot...he liked to be called Lone Wolf..." she laughed, and then continued,"...built the cabin himself."

"Really?"

"Yes. He built it before he and Grandmother got married....actually, even before they met."

"It's pretty old then, isn't it?"

"Yes. It is."

A moment later Janie began giggling.

"What's so funny?" Russ asked, smiling at his wife.

Her giggling turned into laughter.

"What?" Russ asked, looking at Janie.

"I remember Grandmother telling me she made Grandfather put an indoor bathroom in the cabin before she would agree to marry him"

"Did he?" Russ glanced briefly at Janie.

"Oh, don't worry, city boy, you won't have to go outside," Janie said, smiling at her husband. "Yes, of course, he put a bathroom in the cabin."

"Well, thank goodness."

"The bathroom tale was always one of their favorite stories," Janie laughed. "The cabin is getting pretty old now, but Grandmother continues to make improvements on it. Last year she added a couple of rooms."

"Does she mind living alone?"

"No. The cabin was very remote when she and Grandfather first lived there, but through the years more people built houses on the mountain so she has neighbors nearby now."

"That's good."

They rode on in silence for a moment, then Russ looked at Janie and asked, "You did remember to bring your paints and easel, didn't you?"

"Oh, yes, I want to paint some scenes around Grandmother's cabin. The view is spectacular from the front porch. You'll love it!" Janie said. She looked over at Russ and patted him on the knee.

"Can't wait," he smiled at Janie.

"Grandfather planted a Cherokee Rose bush in honor of Grandmother on the day he proposed marriage to her. He planted it in the front yard of the cabin," Janie continued. "It blooms every year."

"It's still alive?"

"Yes. Ask Grandmother to tell you the legend of the Cherokee Rose bush. It's a beautiful Cherokee story."

"I will."

"They had their marriage ceremony on the front porch of the cabin...a Cherokee Traditional Wedding Ceremony," Janie said, then added, "I wish I had been there. It must have been beautiful."

Russ nodded.

"It's too bad that your Grandfather passed before you had more time to spend with him," Russ said softly.

"Yes. He was so talented. Wait until you see his artwork in Grandmother's cabin. It's beautiful."

"I look forward to it."

"My brother was named for him," Janie continued. "You've seen Hunter's paintings. I think he inherited Grandfather's talent."

"Hunter's work is good."

"Yes," Janic answered, smiling. "Grandmother believes his work will be nationally known someday."

Janie turned and glanced at the large cage on the back seat.

"I bet Wa-Yah will enjoy being grandmother's neighbor."

Russ nodded.

"It will be hard to let him go," Janie added.

Russ nodded slowly, remembering how much he loved the animal.

"But now he's too big for us to keep...especially in the city," Janie mused.

"That's true," agreed Russ. "He needs the woods and wild country for his home...a place where he can run free."

"I love him too much to keep him in a pen for the rest of his life," Janie said solemnly, frowning slightly.

Both reflected silently on the enjoyment the animal had brought to them in the short time they had owned him.

Janie looked toward the cage again and smiled.

"We love you, Wa-Yah, enough to set you free," Janie whispered softly, gazing into the animal's blue eyes as he stared back at her.

She turned back to look at the highway and began to sing a Cherokee song. Russ joined in to harmonize in his less than perfect baritone and they laughed at their discord, but declared they made joyous noise together.

Janie glanced at the animal again, then looked back toward the highway and caught her breath. Her eyes widened and she screamed!

On the road in front of them loomed a car passing a very large truck. Both were side by side on the top of the hill, and racing toward them at high rates of speed.

Russ looked to each side of the road quickly, hoping for an escape route, but the ravines bordering the highway were deep and had many trees jutting up among the slopes.

Janie screamed again and threw her hands over her eyes.

She heard brakes screeching...

Metal ripping...

Glass breaking...

And then...nothing.

Janie

TSE-NI (JAY NEE)

OF CHEROKEE

The Great, Great Granddaughter of White Feather

By Nancy McIntosh Pafford

CHAPTER ONE

A soft breeze stirred the leaves on the nearby trees, and then swept across the cabin porch, gently caressing Rose and Tara.

"This has been a beautiful day," Rose said, slowly moving back and forth in the big rocking chair.

"Yes," agreed Tara.

Rose glanced up at the clear blue sky. "Not a cloud in the sky."

"Right...and warm too," nodded Tara, Rose's best friend. She tilted her head back to enjoy the coolness of the breeze drifting across her face.

"Listen," said Rose, "you can hear the water splashing over the rocks in the river."

"I love that sound," Tara said. "I know you must enjoy living so close to the river."

Rose nodded, glancing toward the sparkling water bathed in the sunlight.

The elderly women sat silently for a moment, gazing at the river and enjoying the beauty of the mountains around them.

A flock of chirping birds claimed their attention and they looked up to watch while the birds circled in front of the cabin before they moved on. Their gaze then returned to the river where a pair of ducks watched their four young ducklings playing in the swift current. The wild flowers along the river bank were in full bloom.

"I can hardly wait until Janie and Russ get here...which should be soon...I hope," said Rose.

"It's been a long time since you've seen them, hasn't it?" Tara asked.

"Yes, it has."

"I'm looking forward to seeing Janie again," smiled Tara, "and I'm anxious to meet her husband."

"That's right. You haven't met Russ, have you?" Rose asked.

Tara shook her head.

"And Steve hasn't met Janie or Russ, has he?" Rose asked.

"No," Tara answered, shaking her head.

The two friends continued rocking in silence for a moment.

"How does Steve like his new job with the National Park Service?" Rose asked, breaking the quietness.

"Loves it! He retired from one job and went right into a new one," Tara laughed. "He enjoys being a park ranger."

Rose nodded, and smiled at her friend.

"Tara, do you remember the first time we met...when I came here to teach school?" Rose asked.

"Oh, yes," Tara answered,

"I was so young."

"We were both young then," Tara smiled. "That was a long time ago."

The women laughed softly, remembering the days of their youth.

"And you fell in love with Lone Wolf," Tara reminisced.

"Yes," Rose smiled.

"Everybody in town knew the two of you were meant for each other...even before you realized you were in love with him," Tara teased.

Rose chuckled quietly, and then became silent for a moment.

"He was a good husband," Rose said softly.

"And a good man," added Tara.

"You know, Tara, even after all these years have passed, I still miss Lone Wolf," Rose said, her eyes misting.

"I'm sure you do, Rose."

"Yes," Rose responded quietly.

"He died at such a young age."

Rose nodded.

"He was forty-seven years old, wasn't he?" Tara asked.

Rose nodded again.

The two friends sat quietly for a moment, each lost in their own thoughts of days gone by.

"Now," Rose said brightly, softly clapping her hands together, breaking the silence. "Let's have good thoughts. Let's hope that my beautiful granddaughter and her handsome husband arrive soon."

"Rose, I wish I could stay until they get here, but I need to get home and cook for my husband," Tara said, glancing down at her watch. "He'll be home soon, and he comes in hungry as a bear after his winter sleep," she laughed.

"All right, but you must come over tomorrow and have lunch with us."

"Will do, my friend," Tara laughed. "I never pass up a free meal."

The women rose from their chairs and hugged each other.

"I'll see you tomorrow," Tara said, waving as she opened the door to her car.

Rose watched while Tara's car disappeared down the mountain road. She looked at her watch, and glanced at the road again, hoping to see Janie and Russ arriving. She stood for a moment, sighed deeply, and went into her cabin.

CHAPTER TWO

*T*he bedroom was covered in darkness when the shrill ringing of the telephone awakened Tara and Steve.

Tara sat up in bed, fumbled with the phone in the dark until she found the receiver and put it to her ear.

"Hello," she said sleepily.

"Tara, I'm sorry to wake you, but I know something has happened to Janie and Russ," Rose said nervously.

"Rose?" Tara asked, trying to shake herself awake.

"Tara!" Rose said, her voice rising. "There's something wrong!"

Tara sat up quickly in the bed, reached over and switched on the bedside lamp. She knew something was seriously wrong for her friend to be calling so late and she could hear the strain in Rose's voice.

"Tara, it's after twelve o'clock and they haven't arrived. I've called them on their cell phones over and over and there's no answer on either one of them," Rose said, her words racing.

Steve pushed himself up on his elbow and tapped Tara on the shoulder. "What's going on?" he asked yawning.

"Shh," she answered, putting a finger to her lips. "Rose, are you there?"

"Yes."

"Rose, maybe they decided to stop somewhere and spend the night."

"They would have called me," Rose responded quickly.

"We'll come right over," Tara said, now fearing that

Rose could be right. "We'll be there shortly."

"Thank you," Rose whispered.

"What's happened?" Steve asked, now sitting up in bed and rubbing his eyes.

"Get up. We need to go to Rose," Tara said, throwing off the bed covers. "She is worried because Janie and Russ haven't arrived and she's not been able to reach them by phone."

Quickly Steve and Tara dressed and left for Rose's cabin. When they arrived Rose met them at the door, her face etched in frowns.

"Thank you both for coming," she said, hugging Tara and then Steve. "Something's wrong...I can feel it."

"Have you called anyone who might know something about them?" Steve asked.

"I tried to reach Hunter and Emily but there were no answers at their homes."

"When was the last time you talked to Janie?" Steve asked.

"Hours ago."

"What did she say?" Steve asked.

"She said that they had passed through Ashville and should be here in about an hour."

"Rose, let me make some calls and see if I can find out anything," Steve offered.

"Thank you, Steve," Rose replied.

"I'll go in the bedroom to use the phone," he added over his shoulder as he left the room.

Rose paced the floor and wrung her hands nervously. "Tara..."

"Sit down, Rose," Tara said, putting her arm around Rose's shoulders and leading her to the sofa. "I'll make coffee for us." She patted her friend on the shoulder, and headed for the kitchen.

As Tara entered the kitchen she remembered how she and Rose had spent many happy hours in this cheery room sharing recipes, cooking jelly, tending babies and making good memories. Now, though, the room did nothing to dispel her fears...fears she dared not let her dear friend see until they learned what had happened to her granddaughter and her husband.

Rose sank down on the sofa and rubbed her eyes. She watched her longtime friend leave the room and thought how much she appreciated and treasured the couple's friendship.

"It seems they are always near to help me when I need it," Rose thought, remembering how they had supported her when Lone Wolf died.

Rose had been in shock for days following his sudden, untimely death and Tara and Steve had never left her side.

"Here, drink this," Tara said, returning and handing Rose a cup of coffee. She sat down beside Rose and the two friends sipped their coffee and waited anxiously for Steve to return.

A short time later Steve quietly walked back into the room, his head down. He stood before Rose and looked directly into her eyes. The look he gave her sent chills down Rose's spine and she knew the news was not good.

"Rose," he said quietly.

Looking into his face Rose sensed that something was wrong...terribly wrong.

"What?" she whispered. "What has happened?"

"Rose," he began slowly, "Rose, there's been an accident."

Rose's hand flew to her face. "An accident?" she asked her voice breaking.

Tara reached over and took Rose's hand.

"An automobile accident, Rose. It happened between Ashville and Waynesville."

Rose's face paled as she sank back on the sofa.

"An accident?" she whispered in disbelief. "Janie...Russ?"

Tara took the coffee cup from Rose's shaking hand, and put her arm around her friend.

"We need to go, Rose," Steve said, extending his hand to her. "Come."

"Go?" Rose asked numbly. "Go where?"

"To Ashville. We will take you."

Rose did not move when Tara tried to help her up

from the sofa.

Tara looked at Steve solemnly while her husband shook his head slowly from side to side.

"Are Russ and Janie all right?" Rose asked, looking up at Steve, fearing the answer.

"We're going to find out when we get to the hospital," Steve answered gently. "Come Rose, we must go now."

"Steve...?" Rose asked, her eyes clouded with tears, "...I need to..."

"Come, Rose, let's go," Tara interrupted, again trying to help her friend stand up.

Steve hesitated and looked questionably at Tara.

Tara nodded, then slipped closer to Rose and tightened her arm around her friend's shoulders. "Tell us, Steve, tell us what you found out...please."

"Rose," he began slowly, "Russ didn't survive the accident."

Rose gasped. "NO!" She began breathing rapidly, tears swelling in her eyes. "And...and...Janie?" Rose pleaded for an answer, leaning closer to Steve.

"Rose, Janie is alive, but in critical condition. She's in the trauma unit at the hospital," he answered softly "and will have surgery soon."

Rose began sobbing softly as Tara enfolded her in loving arms while tears streamed down her own face.

"We must hurry," Steve urged. "We need to leave right now."

"Come, Rose," Tara said. "We need to go."

Rose stood slowly, picked up her handbag, and walked toward the front door.

Steve turned out the lights and locked the door behind them. The trio walked slowly out on the porch and down the steps toward the car with Steve and Tara supporting Rose's trembling body between them.

When they reached the car Rose stepped back from Steve so he could open the door for her. She gripped his arm, pushing her fingers deep into the flesh. "Do they think Janie will live?"

Steve did not respond. Instead, he helped Rose and Tara into the car and settled himself, ready to begin the journey..

Rose looked at him and again grabbed his arm.

"Tell me, Steve," she said, raising her voice frantically. "Tell me what you heard. I want to know."

"The hospital called Janie's brother and sister and they are on their way also," he said. "They should be there when we arrive."

"Steve...will she...will she live?" Rose's voice broke, and the frantic tears returned.

He turned and looked at Rose. "We don't know, Rose. The doctors are doing all they can to save her," he responded quietly.

Rose buried her face in her hands and new tears formed in her eyes while Steve started the car and guided it toward the road leading down the mountain.

Tara pulled Rose close to her and whispered, "We are with you, Rose."

In the darkness of the night the three friends traveled down the mountain to face the terrible unknown together and the persistent ringing of the telephone in Rose's cabin went unheard.

CHAPTER THREE

*E*mily and Hunter rushed into a world of pandemonium. They had never been in a trauma unit before and were not prepared for the scene they witnessed.

Men and women in white coats and green scrubs were rushing in every direction shouting orders and tending to the injured. The chaos only added to the nightmare of this tragedy for the brother and sister.

When they reached the nurse's station Hunter identified himself and his sister and they were escorted down a short corridor and into another room.

The room was as bright as the morning sun even at this late hour, but the darkness that hung just outside the window seemed to penetrate the walls and spread its gloom. The room was small and was filled with machines and equipment. It reminded Hunter of something he had seen in a movie about space travel and it made the nightmare become a reality when they saw Janie lying motionless on the bed. Her face was covered in bandages ...only her closed eyes and mouth were visible.

"She is in severe shock, and..." the doctor had said to Hunter and Emily when they arrived at the hospital, "...she has lost a lot of blood. Her leg is broken. She has multiple cuts and bruises on her body...especially her face....and ..."

Emily gasped and began to cry while Hunter stood by his sister's side, unmoving, trying to grasp the doctor's words.

"...her condition is critical," the doctor continued. "She will have surgery for her leg in about an hour or perhaps sooner."

"Doctor, she will live, won't she?" Emily asked anxiously, looking at the doctor through her tears.

"She's young and strong," he responded, patting Emily on the shoulder. "We're going to do everything we can to help her."

Then he turned and quietly left the room, not allowing the young people to see the concern he felt.

Hunter and Emily stood by their sister's bedside, their faces lined in worry. Only the sound of the machines supporting Janie's life broke the silence in the room.

"Will she make it, Emily?" Hunter whispered softly over the lump in his throat.

Emily and Hunter stared at Janie. It seemed so strange seeing their vibrant sister lying so still. Their thoughts jumped rapidly to the hours and days ahead, moving from the immediate concern of surgery to the dread of having to tell Janie that her husband had not survived.

Emily put her arm around her brother's shoulders and shook her head slowly from side to side. She was afraid to speak, fearing that the flowing tears would erupt in loud racking sobs."Only time will tell," she whispered.

Hunter clung to his sister until they were both able to control their fears.

Leaning over Janie, Emily gently stroked her sister's swollen, bruised arm.

"I wish she could open her eyes. Then she would know we are here and she's not alone."

Hunter nodded.

"Grandmother Rose!" Emily said suddenly, turning to Hunter.

"What?"

"Grandmother Rose! They were to arrive at her house late this afternoon. She must be worried...terribly worried!"

"We need to call her right away," Hunter said, turning to leave the room. "I'll do it now."

"No! Don't call Grandmother...call Tara and ask

her to go to Grandmother's house and tell her about the accident."

"Good idea. I won't tell Tara everything...just that Janie and Russ were in an accident."

As Hunter opened the door to leave the room Emily called softly, "Wait!"

She walked to Hunter, took his hand. "Tell Grandmother to come. We need her," she added, her voice breaking.

Hunter nodded, turned and glanced back at Emily.

"We do...we all do," he whispered.

"We need Grandmother Rose...we really need her," Emily whispered to herself as she watched the door slowly close. She walked back to Janie's bed and leaned down close to her sister's face.

"Hang on, Janie, Grandmother Rose will be here soon," she said softly, taking her sister's hand. Then she dropped her head on the pillow beside Janie's head and wept quietly.

CHAPTER FOUR

1993 - Two Years Earlier

*T*hree days before the wedding Janie hurried to meet her Grandmother Rose at the airport, anxious to see her again. When she spied her grandmother Janie ran into her arms and felt like she was being wrapped up with feathery wings...angel wings. She often thought of her grandmother as her guardian angel and she loved her dearly. Even though Rose loved all of her grandchildren Janie was the first and she held a special place in her heart. The bond between them was strong and true.

"I'm so glad you came for our wedding, Grandmother," Janie said excitedly, taking a small tote bag from Rose.

"You didn't think I would miss it....did you?" Rose laughed. "Now stand back," she said, gently pushing Janie away from her, "and let me take a good look at you."

Janie laughed, stepped away and faced her with a broad smile.

"Well, Grandmother, what do you think?" she asked, smiling and putting her hands on her hips.

"Pretty as a picture," Rose said, looking at the tall, slender, dark-haired young woman in front of her. "You still have a smile that's contagious to everyone around you," Rose added, laughing.

"Let me carry that for you, Grandmother," Janie offered, nodding toward the long, slender package Rose carried.

"Thank you for offering, honey," Rose responded,

"but no thanks, I'll carry it."

"What have you got in there? A sword?" Janie teased, looking at the unusual shape of the package.

"No," Rose laughed. "It's your wedding gift!"

A look of surprise crossed Janie's face.

"My wedding gift?"

"Yes."

Janie reached out eagerly toward the package. "Oh, let me see!"

"No...it's for later," Rose said, moving it out of her granddaughter's reach.

"Well, all right," Janie laughed, hugging her grandmother.

"Where's your mother?" Rose asked, looking around. "Didn't she come with you?"

Janie's smile faded and her face became solemn. "I insisted that she wait for us at home. Mother hasn't been feeling well lately, Grandmother."

"Why didn't you let me know?"

"She wouldn't let me. She said she was just tired from the rush of all the wedding plans and activities. But, Grandmother, I'm really worried about her."

"I wish I had known. I could have come earlier to help her."

"Well, you know Mother...Miss Independence. She has promised me she will see a doctor after the wedding."

"Make sure she does," Rose said firmly, as they walked toward the exit of the building.

"I will."

Janie wrapped her arm around Rose's shoulders. "Now, I have someone with me who's very anxious to meet you."

"I wonder who that could be," Rose teased.

"It's Russ, Grandmother..." Janie laughed, "...my finance."

"Well, I'm looking forward to meeting him," Rose chuckled, looking all around. "Where is he?"

"Still trying to find a place to park, I suppose. He said he would meet us in the lobby."

After they retrieved Rose's luggage and headed for

the lobby, Janie saw Russ hurrying toward them, waving his hand wildly in the air.

"Russ!" Janie called, returning his wave.

"I finally found a parking place," he laughed when he reached them.

"Good," Janie responded.

He turned toward Rose and smiled. "Now, this must be Grandmother Rose, the lady I've heard so much about."

"It is!" Janie said with a broad smile, looking at Rose. "Grandmother, this is Russ and Russ, this is Grandmother."

Rose reached out and pulled Russ to her. "Come here, you tall young man. Lean down here so I can give you a hug!" She looked over Russ's shoulder, smiled and winked at Janie. "He's handsome!" she whispered, thinking what beautiful children they would have someday.

"Let me carry those for you," Russ offered, motioning toward her luggage and the package.

"You carry my suitcases...I'll carry this," Rose said, holding up the gift clutched in her hand.

Seeing the curious look on Russ's face while he peered at the strange-looking package Janie leaned close to him and whispered, "The package has a wedding gift in it ...I can't image what it could be...and she won't give it to me now."

"I heard that," Rose teased. "And that's right. You won't get this until the time is right." She shook the package in front of them, laughing.

Janie and Russ looked at each other and shook their heads from side to side, and returned Rose's laughter, all of them enjoying the fun of the moment.

"Let's get out of here. You must be tired, Grandmother," Janie said, taking Rose's arm.

"A little, but I want to hear all about this upcoming wedding and I'm anxious to see my daughter and other grandchildren too."

CHAPTER FIVE

*R*uth was dozing on the sofa when Rose and Janie arrived and did not get up to greet them.

Rose rushed over and hugged her daughter and was surprised at the amount of weight she had lost since their last visit together. With concern showing on her face and in her voice Rose asked, "Ruth, aren't you feeling well?"

"Oh, just a little tired," Ruth smiled.

"Well, weddings can be a strain...with all the activity," Rose said, patting her daughter's hand and sitting down beside her.

"Actually, Janie has done almost everything."

"That's good," Rose smiled.

"Have you met Russ?" asked Ruth.

"Yes," said Rose, smiling.

"He's a fine young man. We love him and we're glad he is going to be part of our family."

Rose nodded.

"Have you been to the doctor for a check-up lately, Ruth?" Rose asked, changing the subject.

"No. Why do you ask?"

"Oh, I just thought that you look tired and might like to get a check up... you know, to see if you need some vitamins or something," Rose said, trying to sound casual and unalarmed.

"I'll go after the wedding."

The door swung open suddenly.

Emily and Hunter rushed into the room, each trying to be first to hug their grandmother.

"Oh, my beautiful grandchildren!" Rose declared with all their arms around her. "Now back up and let me take a good look at the two of you."

They stepped away from Rose, both smiling at their grandmother. Emily struck a silly pose and laughed while Hunter stretched his shoulders up to show how much he had grown. Then they pulled chairs close to their grandmother, sat down and tried to catch her up on news about the things they had been doing since the last time she had seen them.

Rose sat, looking at her grandchildren, and thinking about how fast they were growing into adults.

Hunter, named for his grandfather, had grown taller since she had seen him the last time. He reminded her so much of Lone Wolf. He wore his black hair in the same style her husband had done. It was short on the sides, with long hair pulled to the back in a pony tail. His dark eyes crinkled when he smiled like his grandfather had done.

"Oh," Rose thought. "I have missed my husband's smile so many times. Now I see it again on Hunter's face."

Hunter was becoming a very accomplished artist and it made Rose happy to hear that he was serious about his work. Rose hoped that he would attend college or art school when he graduated from high school. And, smiling broadly, Hunter showed his grandmother a picture of his new girlfriend.

Rose glanced at her granddaughter, sixteen year old Emily...sweet little Emily...small, petite, and always smiling. She learned that Emily was eager to learn more about her Cherokee heritage and culture which greatly pleased Rose   Emily's only flaw seemed to be her lack of patience. The entire family recognized and tolerated her impatience and often teased her about it. She had a boyfriend and Emily thought that he was the person she would marry someday.

"Grandmother, he's wonderful," Emily swooned as she leaned closer to Rose.

"Ah, youth," thought Rose, smiling at Emily, "always in love."

The next day was a whirl of activity and Rose was enjoying all of it... helping out where she was needed and watching the rush of everyone getting ready for the wedding the following day.

After a short nap during the afternoon, Rose walked down the hall to Janie's room and knocked on the door.

"Come in," sang out a happy Janie.

Rose eased the door open and peeped into her room. Across the room she saw Janie putting on a dress in front of the full length mirror, then looking at herself.

"Hey, Grandmother. Come in," Janie called over her shoulder.

Emily was lying in the middle of the bed on her stomach, elbows bent to support her head. She was watching her sister intently with a wistful look on her face.

"Come sit by me, Grandmother," Emily said, sitting up and patting the bed beside her. "Let's watch the bride!" she added, laughing.

Rose joined in the laughter, glad to be a part of this happy occasion. "Where is your mother, girls?" Rose asked, sitting down on the bed beside Emily.

"At the church," answered Emily, "She's checking on everything. She's feeling much better today."

"Good," said Rose.

"And where are the men?" Rose asked. "It's very quiet in the house."

"Hunter and Russ went to pick up their tuxedos for the wedding tomorrow. They will meet us at the church for the wedding rehearsal and dinner tonight," Janie said, while she turned in a circle admiring her new dress.

"We're all so glad you're here, Grandmother," Emily said, putting her arm around Rose.

"I wouldn't miss this wedding!" Rose smiled. "Russ is a lucky man."

"Good looking, too," laughed Emily.

"Well, I'm ready," Janie said, turning to face Emily and Rose.

"FINALLY!" Emily said.

"Do I look all right?" Janie asked.

"Yes, you look fine," Emily said, standing up.

"Now, can we can go?"

"Yes," Janie nodded to her sister.

"FINALLY!" Emily repeated in an exasperated tone.

"Oh, sister...just wait until you get married. You'll know why I'm so nervous and want everything to be perfect," Janie said good-naturally.

"After seeing all this carrying on...I'm going to ELOPE!" Emily said.

Rose and Janie laughed.

"I've been wondering about that package you brought with you, Grandmother...the one you wouldn't let me carry at the airport." Janie said.

"What package?" Emily asked, a little louder.

"You two are so curious...always have been.The package is put away until the time is right," smiled Rose.

"What package?" Emily insisted.

"Grandmother brought it with her. It's a wedding gift," Janie said, "and she won't give it to me," she added, giving Rose a playful push on the shoulder.

"Oh, you'll get it tomorrow...don't worry," Rose smiled.

"Grandmother, let us see it," begged Emily.

"You two girls are too curious. Janie will get it tomorrow...don't worry."

"Please," chimed both of the girls together.

"Yes, please," Emily begged, while she placed her hands together in a prayer position.

"Tomorrow...I promise," Rose said again, chuckling, amused and feeling pleasure to be able to share this exciting time with her family. Her only regret was that Lone Wolf was not here to share it with her. With that thought a warm feeling passed over her and she knew that indeed he was here.

CHAPTER SIX

*T*he big day for the wedding had arrived and everyone in the house was looking forward to the marriage ceremony and celebration that would take place soon.

The rooms in Ruth's house echoed with loud talking and laughter among the family members as everyone prepared for the wedding. Rose observed everything, watching and listening with amusement and pleasure.

"EMILY!!!" Hunter yelled in a loud voice from his room.

"WHAT?" she yelled back.

"EMILY! COME HERE!" Hunter's voice rang out through the house.

"What?" Emily demanded, coming to the door of Hunter's room. She stood in the doorway in her bare feet and showed her disgust with her hands on her hips. "What do you want?"

"I can't find my black socks anywhere!" Hunter yelled as he searched through his sock drawer, tossing one pair of socks after another over his shoulder, flinging them carelessly to the floor. "I have a good pair of blue socks, but I can't wear them with a black tuxedo!"

"No! You can't!"

"Well, what am I going to do?"

"Oh! Go to the store and buy a pair!" Emily told him impatiently, rolling her eyes upward and turning to leave the room.

"I don't have time!"

"Keep looking!" she yelled back at him over her shoulder. "Oh! Men!" she said, throwing her hands up in the air as she flounced down the hall.

"Both of you stop that yelling!" Janie called from the door of her room. "Mother is trying to rest."

Emily rushed back to her room and slammed the door. She took off her robe, quickly grabbed her bridesmaid dress from the hanger and flung it over her head.

"Oh, no!" she moaned, tugging and pulling at the dress.

"Grandmother!" she called loudly, rushing to open the door. "Grandmother, can you come in here a minute, please?"

"What's the matter?" Rose asked, hurrying into the room.

"This dress! Look!" she said, turning to show the dress open down the back. "The zipper broke!"

"No problem," Rose assured her. "Take off the dress. I'll fix the zipper."

"Thank you, Grandmother," Emily said as she quickly slipped the dress over her head and handed it to Rose.

Rose took the dress, put it over her arm and started out of the room.

When Emily glanced into the mirror she groaned again.

"What's the matter now?" Rose asked, turning to face Emily.

"Now I've messed up my hair. I'll have to do it all over again."

Rose left the room smiling and shaking her head. She was enjoying being involved in the entire scene. "This is the way it's meant to be on the day of a wedding, I suppose," she assured herself with a chuckle.

She repaired the dress in short time and was ready to return it to Emily when she heard Hunter and Emily talking loudly to each other. She paused to listen, smiling.

"Well, I'm just going to wear blue socks!" Hunter snorted.

"Well...I don't care!" Emily shot back at him, putting her hands on her hips. "Nobody's going to look at you anyway."

"The sock war's still on, I hear," Rose said softly. She laughed, thinking that she wouldn't have missed all of this activity for anything.

Meanwhile in another room all was quiet.

After solving the small problems of the day, Rose slipped quietly into Ruth's bedroom and sat down on the bed beside her.

"How are you feeling today, Ruth?" Rose asked softly.

Ruth opened her eyes and smiled weakly at Rose. "Just a little tired...the wedding and all, you know."

"Janie told me that you haven't been feeling well for a long time."

"Oh well," Ruth said, dismissing Janie's comment, "I'm not getting any younger, Mother."

"Ruth, I want you to see a doctor next week. I'm going to stay here with you and see that you get a checkup as soon as possible."

"No, Mother, you go home. I promise I'll see a doctor."

"Promise?"

"Yes."

Rose leaned over the bed and kissed her daughter. "Now rest. I'll come back in a little while and help you get ready for the wedding...and don't worry. I'll get this show on the road," Rose laughed.

Ruth smiled as her mother disappeared from the room. She sighed, rubbed the ache in her left arm and closed her eyes. "Just a few more minutes," she thought.

CHAPTER SEVEN

Rose had anxiously watched the clock for the past hour. Now it was one hour before the wedding ceremony...the time she had been waiting for all day...the time she had planned to talk with Janie alone. Walking quietly down the hall she paused at the open door to her granddaughter's room.

Janie was standing before the mirror and the sight of her beauty caused Rose to catch her breath. She was dressed in a long ivory-colored satin wedding gown adorned with lace and seed pearls. Janie's dark hair, piled loosely on top of her head, was crowned with a circle of flowers with a short veil trailing down her back.

"You look beautiful, Janie," Rose whispered slowly, her eyes clouding. "You are the most beautiful bride I have ever seen."

Janie turned at the sound of Rose's voice.

"Thank you, Grandmother," she said, smiling at Rose.

"So beautiful...." Rose said softly, her eyes misting with love for her grandchild.

"Come in, please," invited Janie, smiling at her grandmother.

"Do you have time to come to my room for a minute before we leave for the church, Janie?"

"Yes, of course."

Janie gathered the long skirt of her wedding gown in her hands, then pulled it up above her ankles and followed Rose down the hall.

After they entered Rose's room she put her hands on Janie's shoulders and turned the young woman toward her. She looked deeply into Janie's dark eyes.

31

"I want to give you your wedding present," Rose said softly. "It is time."

"But, Grandmother, you have already given us a present," Janie said, temporarily forgetting the mysterious package that Rose had brought with her.

"I know," Rose replied, nodding her head. She walked over to the bed and sat down. "This one is just for you."

"Oh, that's right! I had forgotten...you know, with all the excitement."

Rose looked at her granddaughter and smiled. "Now you are all grown up and getting married..."

"Yes," Janie interrupted with a return smile.

"...and I am happy for you."

"Thank you."

"You know..." Rose began slowly, "...marriage has its happy times and sad times too...and times when you will need to be very strong."

"Like you, Grandmother, when you were lost in the woods. You were so brave."

Rose nodded slowly.

"Janie, do you ever think about the little cemetery in Georgia...the one we visited when you were a young girl?" Rose asked.

"Oh, yes...I do. We saw our Cherokee ancestors' graves. I remember...especially the one that belonged to Great, Great Grandmother White Feather."

"Do you recall our conversation when we were leaving the cemetery that day?" Rose asked.

"Yes."

"When we started back to the car you stopped me and said that you could feel Grandmother White Feather's spirit...you said you felt that her spirit was like wings around you."

"Oh...yes. I remember," Janie smiled. "Yes, I know that her spirit was with me that day. I felt the power of love pass down to me from her."

Rose nodded.

"I've thought about that many times since then," Janie said softly.

"When we hugged at the airport I felt the wings of

her spirit had brushed my cheek. It was the same feeling you had many years ago when I told you the story of White Feather," Rose said softly.

Janie moved closer to her grandmother, never taking her gaze away from Rose's eyes, and then sat down on the edge of the bed beside her.

Rose placed her hands on her granddaughter's shoulders. "Janie, many years ago when I was abducted and then lost in the woods I knew that White Feather's spirit was with me. I felt the power of love all around me," said Rose. "One day you will need strength too....the spirit of strength and love passed on to me from White Feather. Now I want to pass it on to you"

Janie remembered her Grandmother Rose telling about her Cherokee heritage and her eyes misted as she looked at the grandmother she loved so dearly. The legacy of her ancestors now held new meaning and again she felt the warm sensation of love surrounding her like wings enfolding her in their soft down.

Rose stood and went to the closet and opened the door. She took out the package that had been kept a secret from Janie. She paused, looked at her granddaughter, and then walked slowly and stood before her.

"Here, open it," she whispered. "This belongs to you now."

Slowly Janie took the package and striped away the paper. She gasped, and looked quickly at her grandmother. "Grandmother! The hiking stick!"

"Yes," Rose smiled.

"This is the one that Great Grandfather Walking Eagle gave you...the one you showed me when I visited you."

Rose nodded and sat down beside her granddaughter. "Now it is yours."

"What a wonderful gift," Janie said, turning it over and over in her hands, running her fingers over the carved white feathers and Cherokee Roses. She looked up at her grandmother, her eyes brimming with tears.

"It is very, very old," said Rose. "Red Fox carved it and gave it to White Feather. When she died her daughter, Little Fawn, kept the stick and later, when she became an old woman, she passed it on to your Great Grandfather, Walking Eagle. He gave it to me when I was very young...when he discovered that I was a Cherokee. I received it not long before I married your Grandfather, Lone Wolf."

Janie's gaze never left the stick while her grandmother spoke.

Rose wrapped her fingers around Janie's hands on the stick and smiled at her granddaughter fondly.

Janie could feel the warmth of her grandmother's fingers wrapped around her hands. The bond of their spirits was powerful. Her eyes sought Rose's gaze and their eyes locked.

"We are Cherokee women, Janie. Don't ever forget we are strong. Remember the women before you who have held this stick. The stick cannot give you power...instead it serves as a symbol of the strength of the women who have owned it. It should always be kept as a reminder that they overcome life threatening challenges. They faced them with strength, determination and perseverance in order to survive."

The emotion in her grandmother's voice was like a warning, but the strength of her words was a promise.

Janie nodded slowly while she felt again the whisper of a quiet spirit of long ago.

"My wish for you is that you will always be as happy as you are today, Janie, but along life's way you might face challenging times also. Remember your ancestors. Don't ever forget."

"I won't, Grandmother," Janie whispered respectfully. "I won't."

Rose smiled, leaned forward and kissed her granddaughter on the cheek.

"Grandmother, I will treasure this stick forever. Thank you." Janie said, pulling the stick close to her body where it lay against the beating of her heart.

Rose smiled. "Come, now, it's time to go."

Janie continued to hold the stick against her

body, then stood and went into her grandmother's outstretched arms with tears in her eyes. The stick touched both the Cherokee women's hearts as it rested between them and they both felt the embrace of wings.

"No crying, now," Rose said brightly, pulling away from Janie. "We've got a wedding to attend."

Janie nodded, smiled at Rose and then carefully laid the stick on her grandmother's bed.

"Now go!" Rose laughed. She put her hands on Janie's shoulders, and turned her toward the door.

As Janie walked out into the hall Rose gave her a playful slap on the backside. "Scat!"

Janie laughed. "Take care of my hiking stick until I get back!" she added over her shoulder.

Watching her granddaughter disappear down the hall Rose wiped her misty eyes and whispered softly. "Be happy, my darling, be happy."

And then she thought of her husband, Lone Wolf, and how much she wished he was here to share this day with her.

The rustling of the leaves outside her window were like an answer to the wish and she could almost hear him whisper softly, "I am, my love, I am."

CHAPTER EIGHT

*R*ose gazed out the small window of the airplane and watched while the plane glided its way through the thick white clouds preparing to land. When the plane circled the airport and dropped down onto the runway Rose was glad. This first glimpse of her beloved mountains was spectacular. The trees had turned to shades of yellow and red with hues of green dotted with the shadows of the clouds. It reminded her of Hunter and Janie's paint palettes after they finished a canvas. Rose smiled as she thought of her grandchildren and the time she had spent with them, but she was worried about Ruth. She planned to call her later in the week to be sure she had seen her doctor. Spending time with her family and attending the wedding had been enjoyable, but exhausting. Now she was ready to be home again. Stepping out of the plane Rose paused at the door to look up at the tall mountains in the distance. A little smile played across her face.

"They seem to be welcoming me home," she thought while gazing up at them. She retrieved her luggage and hurried into the waiting area. Looking around she immediately saw Tara waving and hurrying toward her.

The two friends rushed to each other and hugged like schoolgirls, giggling in their excitement.

"I missed you!" Tara exclaimed.

"And I missed you. Thanks for coming to pick me up."

"Glad to do it, Rose. Let's get out of here so we can talk. I want to hear all about the wedding."

When they settled themselves in the car, Tara

turned to Rose.

"Now, tell me all about your trip," Tara said, start-
ing the car and moving out of the airport parking lot.
"I want to hear everything."

"Tara, Janie was the most beautiful bride I have
ever seen...and the wedding was beautiful too," Rose
laughed. "It was perfect, except..." she added chuckling, "...except for Hunter's socks!"

"Hunter's socks?"

"Yes. He was in the wedding, of course. He gave
the bride away. But he couldn't find his black socks
to wear with his black tuxedo."

"So?"

"When he realized he didn't have black socks to
wear there wasn't enough time before the wedding for
him to go to a store and buy a pair," Rose said, snick-
ering.

"So what did he wear?"

"BRIGHT BLUE ARGYLE SOCKS!" Rose burst out
laughing.

"Bright blue argyles?"

Rose nodded.

"No, he didn't," Tara hooted.

"Yes!"

"OH, NO!" Tara groaned, and then laughed along
with Rose.

"And the worst part of it was that Emily kept
pointing them out to almost everybody at the recep-
tion," Rose laughed.

Tara continued to laugh, shaking her head from
side to side. "I wish I could have been there."

"Well, it was quite a sight!"

"And how was Ruth?" Tara asked when the two
women settled down and stopped laughing.

Rose suddenly became quiet as a frown crossed
her face. For a moment she didn't speak.

"She's not well, Tara. She's pale and tired all of
the time. I wanted to stay with her for a while, but
she insisted that I return home. She promised me she
would see a doctor next week."

Tara shook her head slowly. "I'm so sorry, Rose."

"I'm really worried about her, Tara," Rose said seriously.

"Maybe she's just tired," Tara said softly, trying to reassure her friend.

The women remained silent for a while, each thinking about Ruth and hoping Tara was right. Other thoughts ran through their minds as they enjoyed the ride and the beautiful vistas before them. They had been friends for so long that they were comfortable with the quiet moments between them.

Tara finally broke the silence.

"Rose, did Ruth ever find out exactly what happened to her husband?"

"No..." Rose said slowly, "...only that he disappeared and was never found. Ruth always felt that Don was dead. Did I ever tell you how he left Ruth?"

Tara shook her head, remembering that she and Steve were away on vacation at the time of his disappearance. When they returned Ruth and the children had gone back to Kentucky and Rose did not speak much about the incident.

"I guess I've never wanted to talk about it because it was so sad," Rose began softly. "It happened a long time ago. Janie was six years old, Hunter, four, and Emily was just a baby. Ruth and Don and the children had come down from Kentucky for a visit with me. After a couple of days they decided to go camping in the mountains. Ruth told me that they spent a night in the woods, sleeping in their tent and cooking over an open fire. They were having a good time and everything was normal and happy."

Rose paused, took a deep breath and continued the story.

"Late in the afternoon of their second day out in the mountains, Don told Ruth that he was going for a hike. He stuffed food in his back pack...which Ruth thought was odd... but he told her he was taking food to eat in case he got hungry. He kissed Ruth and the children and left. When he had not returned by seven o'clock that night Ruth became very worried. She drove to the nearest park ranger station and reported that he had not returned. She and the children went back to the camp and waited. Park rangers and rescue workers searched all night and the next day without finding him. One of the rangers suggested that Ruth pack up their camp, take the children and return to my house while the search continued...which they did. The weather became bad. Heavy rains began and halted the search for a day and a half, but after the rain stopped the rescuers continued looking for Don."

Rose paused, looked out of the window for a moment, and then continued.

"There were many speculations as to what could have happened to him - horror stories of bear attacks, starvation, dehydration or his falling into a deep ravine. Eventually the search was terminated and finally Ruth faced the reality that Don was gone. She went back to Kentucky and worked hard rearing her small children alone. She worked two jobs most of the time...and...well, you know the rest of the story."

Tara nodded her head. "That is so sad, especially for the children," she said.

"I think Janie probably remembers him, but it happened a very long time ago."

Tara nodded again.

"If Ruth doesn't feel well soon I'm going back to be with her. I'm so worried about her health. The children think that she will be fine once she has rested and gotten over all the activity of the wedding. They think their mother just needs rest and then she will get well."

The children were wrong.

Two weeks after the wedding Ruth died in her sleep of a massive heart attack.

*E*verybody, please leave," Rose said after the medical staff had come and taken Janie to surgery. "I will stay here."

"No. Steve and I will stay. You go and get some rest, Rose," Tara said, walking to Rose and putting her arm around her friend's shoulders.

"No," Rose said firmly, glancing at the others in the room. "All of you go. I'll be here. Janie will be in surgery for a long time."

"But, Rose..." Tara began.

"Tara, there's nothing we can do now but pray and wait," Rose interrupted. "The surgery will take a long time. Please go. Steve needs to go to work."

"All right. I will take Steve home and then I'll be back as soon as I can get here," Tara said.

Rose nodded. "Thank you, Tara."

"Rose, do you want me to bring back anything for you...clothes...?"

"Yes," Rose interrupted, "I'm not leaving."

"Is there something I can do for you at home, Rose?" Steve asked.

"No, but thank you for asking," replied Rose.

"I'll be back soon," Tara whispered to Rose as she hugged her.

Before they left Steve and Tara hugged Emily and Hunter, then quietly left the room.

Emily and Hunter continued to argue that they would remain at the hospital but Rose finally convinced them to go to a motel and rest. It had been a nightmare ride from their homes to the hospital and they looked exhausted.

"Go," she told them with a gentle push toward the door. "I might need you tomorrow."

Still reluctant to leave, Rose nudged them out into the hall. "I have your cell phone numbers. I promise I will call you if there is a change. Come back after you have slept for a while."

"But, Grandmother…" Emily said.

"Hush," Rose interrupted, "now go."

After they left Rose walked to a large comfortable-looking chair in the corner of the room and sank down in it. She sighed heavily, closed her eyes and fell asleep immediately. Unsettling dreams disturbed her rest and she awoke with a start and looked at the empty bed. Janie had not been returned to the room. She stood, stretched her arms and walked to the window and watched the sun rise from behind the tall mountains. She rubbed her eyes, then glanced down at her watch and realized that Janie had been out of the room for hours. She yawned as exhaustion overtook her tired body. She sat back down in the chair and closed her eyes again.

Suddenly the door swung open and Rose awoke immediately at the sound of movement in the room. She stood up and watched while Janie was returned to the room and placed in her bed. As soon as the attendants left she hurried to Janie's bedside. She looked down at her granddaughter's leg and bandaged face and caught her breath. She took Janie's hand and caressed it while tears formed in her eyes.

"Oh, my darling," she whispered, stroking Janie's hair with her other hand. "You must be strong and brave for what's ahead of you."

CHAPTER TEN

*T*he morning following surgery Janie's eyelids fluttered slightly, and then remained closed.

The family had waited anxiously for her to wake and they jumped to their feet and hurried to the bed. They stood and waited, speaking softly to her, but Janie didn't stir again.

Several hours later her eyelids opened and a shadow of pain quickly appeared in her eyes that were surrounded by bandages. And again they closed.

Rose sprang to the bedside again and leaned over Janie and waited. She again spoke encouraging words to her hoping for a sign of recognition. But there was no response from Janie.

Later that afternoon a moan escaped from Janie's lips and she opened her eyes and this time they stayed open for a short moment. Her hands trembled as they went slowly to her bandaged face. She covered her eyes with her hands and then tried to speak.

Rose leaned close to her granddaughter and whispered softly as she stroked Janie's hair. "Shh. Don't try to talk now, darling. There will be time later."

Janie closed her eyes and returned to a deep sleep while Rose shook her head from side to side, wondering if her grandchild would live.

Tara had returned to the hospital and she went to Rose and put her arm around her friend. She knew how deeply Rose loved Janie and how much she was suffering. Tara wanted to assure Rose that her granddaughter would be fine but she couldn't give her false hope. The waiting and uncertainly was hard for all of them. They could only hope and pray that Janie would recover.

Hours later Rose, Emily and Hunter were at Janie's bedside when she slowly opened her eyes again. This time she kept them open and tried to focus on the people around her in the room

"Hello, darling," her grandmother said, smiling at Janie with relief sounding in her voice.

"Hey, sis," Hunter said softly as he kissed her bandaged head.

"Hello," Emily's voice broke as she tried to talk to her sister.

"What happened?" Janie asked weakly.

"We'll talk later, after you've rested," Rose said gently.

"No. I want to know now."

Rose shook her head and glanced at the people in the room.

"What happened, Grandmother?" Janie mumbled.

"Let's wait to talk until you are stronger," Rose said soothingly. "You should rest now."

"No! I want to know!" Janie insisted, becoming agitated.

Realizing that Janie was not going to stop questioning, Rose knew that she must be truthful with her granddaughter.

"There was an automobile accident, honey...a very bad one," whispered Rose, leaning down close to her granddaughter.

"Where is Russ?" Janie asked weakly, gazing around the room.

"Shh," Rose whispered over the lump in her throat.

"Where is he?" she asked again, trying to raise her head up from the pillow.

Silence filled the room

Hunter and Emily looked away from Janie, not letting their sister see their tear filled eyes. Hunter shifted his feet and looked down at the floor while Emily turned her back.

Janie searched Rose's face anxiously waiting for an answer. She could feel the tension in the room and she began to panic.

"Is he all right?" she murmured, looking at Rose, her voice begging for an answer to relieve her fears.

Emily leaned close to Rose and whispered. "Grandmother, tell her, please. She needs to know."

Rose cleared her throat and began. "Darling, it was a terrible accident, a wreck between your automobile and a big truck."

"A wreck?" Janie's eyes widened.

Rose nodded, then took a big breath and continued.

"Janie, two people were killed and two survived the crash," she answered softly.

"Two people survived?" Janie's voice mingled with hope and fear.

She looked into her grandmother's face and their eyes locked.

"Yes," Rose nodded, hoping that the tears would not overflow onto her face while she continued. She had dreaded this moment.

"Russ and me?" Janie whispered, lifting her head slightly off the pillow.

The silence in the room was almost deafening.

"Russ?" Janie asked again, scanning the faces of the people around her, panic in her eyes and voice.

Rose slipped her arm around Janie's shoulder and pulled her granddaughter into her arms.

"Russ didn't make it, honey," she said softly.

"What?" Janie stammered. "Russ is dead?"

Rose nodded.

"Russ is dead?" Janie repeated while her hands began to tremble.

"Yes," Rose nodded, fighting back the tears.

Emily began sobbing quietly.

Hunter went to his sister and put his arm around her while fighting back the tears threatening to overflow from his eyes also.

Silent tears flowed down Tara's face while she walked to Hunter and Emily and put an arm around each one and hugged them close to her.

Janie looked at her grandmother in disbelief.

"NO!" she said, shaking her head. "Russ is not

dead! That can't be true!" Her voice rose with every word.

Rose nodded again.

"NO! NO! NO!" Janie screamed loudly.

Rose gently rocked her granddaughter in her arms, holding her close as the realization penetrated the haze of anesthesia.

"RUSS! RUSS!" Janie sobbed loudly, the pain in her voice echoing through the room. "OH! RUSS!"

The door swung open quickly and a young nurse rushed into the room. She took Janie's hand while Rose stepped back from the bed and wiped her tears with the back of her hand.

"The doctor has left an order for a sedative for her," the nurse turned to Rose and whispered. "I'll be right back."

Rose nodded while she pulled Janie into her arms again.

When the nurse returned she gave Janie an injection and motioned for Rose to follow her to the other side of the room.

"The medication will help relax her," she said.

"Thank you," Rose whispered.

"Have you told her everything?" the nurse asked, glancing over at Hunter and Emily at their sister's bedside.

Rose shook her head. "No," she whispered.

"I'll be back soon. My name is Millie. Please ask for me."

The nurse quietly left the room, softly closing the door behind her, her own heart aching for the young woman in her care.

Soon the medication relaxed Janie and her racking sobs changed to quiet tears.

"Grandmother," she said, tracing her hand across her stomach, "is my baby all right?"

Rose knew that she must tell Janie everything. She also knew that it was going to be hard...very hard.

"My baby, Grandmother?"

"Janie, darling, the doctors couldn't save the baby," Rose said softly, remembering her own tears when the doctor had told her earlier. "I'm sorry."

A new flood of tears rolled down Janie's face, soaking the bandages. Tears of defeat at hearing this last devastating news became a realization.

"My poor baby...my baby...my baby," she cried in despair, cradling her stomach as if to protect the already lost baby.

Rose, Tara, Hunter and Emily stood helpless, with tears flowing openly now.

After a short time the medication mercifully lulled Janie back to sleep and Rose stepped away from the bed and sighed, thoroughly exhausted.

Tara went to her friend and gathered her into her arms while the two women cried softly. No words were needed. Their love for each other had formed a bond that spoke much louder than words and they each comforted the other.

Slowly Rose began to recover from the after math of the emotional trauma of worry for Janie's life and now for her recovering not only from injuries from the accident but also from the loss of her husband and unborn child. She knew Janie would need all the strength of her ancestors to survive this tragedy and to have the will to live. Rose knew what it was like to lose a much loved husband and could only imagine the horror of losing an unborn child as well. She moved away from Tara, dried her tears and straightened her shoulders. She motioned for Emily to follow her into the hall.

"Emily, there's something I want you to do," Rose whispered.

"What?"

"I want you to go to Janie's house and get the hiking stick and bring it to the hospital."

"The hiking stick?"

"Yes," Rose said seriously.

"All right. I'll leave now and be back soon," Emily replied, wondering why her grandmother would want the stick at the hospital.

Rose went back to Janie's bedside, looked into her granddaughter's face, and whispered in her ear.

"You must be strong now, Janie...be strong,"

CHAPTER ELEVEN

The long days at the hospital stretched into a week and each day brought healing to Janie's body. To everyone's relief it became apparent that she would recover from her wounds, but it was also apparent that she grew more despondent and emotionally unstable.

Each day Janie's feeling of the loss of Russ and the baby became more painful, and then her pain changed into anger. Her outbursts of anger or sadness resulted in her attacking everyone near her...depending on her mood resulting from her hurting heart.

Millie visited Janie often and had become a friend to Janie's family...especially Rose.

One night Millie eased the door open to Janie's room and found Rose nodding in a chair. She went quietly to Janie's bed and saw that Janie was sleeping.

"Hello, Millie," Rose said wearily.

"I see that Janie is resting," Millie said.

"Yes," Rose responded softly.

"Miss Rose, you are so tired," Millie said, putting her hand on Rose's shoulder. "Why don't you go to the motel and sleep tonight?"

"I don't want Janie to be alone."

"I'll stay with Janie. You can rest and come back in the morning."

"Are you sure you don't mind, Millie?" Rose said, easing herself up tiredly from the chair.

"No," Millie responded with a smile. "Go...Janie will be fine."

"Thank you, Millie. I could use a little rest."

After Rose left, Millie settled herself in a chair beside Janie's bed and closed her eyes.

"What do you want?" Janie snarled out at the young nurse.

"Oh, you're awake," Millie said, opening her eyes.

"Yes! I'm awake!" Janie said sarcastically. "What do you want?"

"I came to visit you," Millie replied pleasantly.

"I don't want any visitors," Janie said angrily.

"Well, you got one anyway," Millie laughed, rising from the chair.

Janie turned her head away from Millie and closed her eyes. "Get out of here and leave me alone!" Janie snapped.

"Janie, please let me..." Millie said, straightening the blanket on the bed.

"Leave!" Janie interrupted.

"Janie, you're going to get better every day, you know," Millie assured Janie.

"I don't care what happens...I have nothing to live for...I..."

"Janie, don't talk that way."

"I said...," Janie said slowly and deliberately, "get out of here!"

Millie walked to the door and left quietly without saying anything else. Later she slipped back into the room as soon as Janie drifted into sleep.

Around daylight the morning sun brightened Janie's room and cast its rays across Millie, arousing her from sleep. She stood, stretched her arms over her head, and muffled a yawn. Before she could ease herself quietly out of the room the door slowly opened.

"Good morning," Rose whispered.

"Good morning," Millie responded, surprised that Rose had returned to the hospital so early in the morning.

"How was the night?" Rose inquired, indicating Janie.

Millie motioned to Rose to follow her out into the hall where they could talk.

"She was restless. She kept calling Russ's name

over and over."

"Poor thing," Rose said sadly.

"And, Miss Rose, she kept murmuring other words...words that sounded like they were in a foreign language."

"Do you remember any of the words?"

"Well, the one she called out most often was Wa-Yah...or something like that," replied Millie.

Rose smiled. "She was calling her pet wolf."

"A pet wolf?"

"Yes. She and Russ had raised it from a pup. They had named it Wa-Yah which is the Cherokee word for wolf."

"How in the world did they happen to get a wolf for a pet?" Millie asked in surprise.

"Russ went into the woods to hunt and as he was leaving to go home he walked up on a mother wolf, her dead body imprisoned in a steel trap. Her pups were scattered around on the ground near their mother, apparently dead also."

Millie listened intently and frowned when she heard about the trap.

"Russ thought that it was horrible, thinking that the little ones had probably died from starvation. Just as he turned to leave the death scene he heard a low whimper and glimpsed a slight movement of one of the pups as it raised its head weakly and looked toward him. It tried to plea for help but no sound escaped from its open mouth. Russ quickly gathered up the trembling pup and gently tucked it under his coat. When he got home and showed the pup to Janie it was love at first sight. They raised him and were bringing him to my house to release him into the woods as he had grown too big for the cage."

"What happened to him?"

"We don't know. Emily asked the ambulance medics about Wa-Yah after the accident and they told her that the door to the cage was open but the cage was empty when they arrived on the scene."

"Poor Wa-Yah," Millie said slowly. "I wonder if he is alive."

"We have no idea what happened to him after the wreck."

"Does Janie know?"

"Yes. When she asked about him Emily told her he could not be found."

Millie shook her head sadly. "Poor Janie," she thought. "One more death to mourn."

Rose took Millie's hand and looked deep into her soft brown eyes.

"Thank you, Millie for all the kindnesses you have shown us."

"I want her to get well," she smiled at Rose.

"She will have the strength to overcome this tragedy."

As Millie left the hospital she couldn't help wondering what Rose had meant by this strange statement, but at the same time she felt a new assurance that Rose's words were true. When she looked up into the bright sunlight of the new day a soft breeze moved around her and she noticed a beautiful white feather drifting toward Janie's window.

CHAPTER TWELVE

*G*ood morning."

Janie slowly opened her eyes and frowned. Her gaze followed the voice and she saw a man in a white coat standing at the foot of her bed.

"How are you feeling today?" he asked, looking over the little glasses perched on the end of his nose.

"How do I know? I'm not awake yet," she murmured slowly with a sigh.

"I'm Dr. Tremont. We haven't spoken," he smiled, "but I've been in to see you every day. This is the first time I've found you awake."

"I wasn't awake," Janie thought sarcastically.

Janie's eyes slowly focused on the face of the man now standing beside her bed.

"Um..m..." he said thoughtfully, flipping through Janie's medical chart. "I see that you've made some good improvements during the past few days."

"Sure, you can tell by just looking at me," she muttered, waving her hand over her broken leg.

"Your leg will heal and so will your face," the doctor responded softly, while he wrote on the chart.

"Oh, sure," Janie flung back at him.

"You are very fortunate to be alive," Dr. Tremont said seriously, removing his glasses and looking straight into Janie's troubled eyes.

"He has a lot of nerve," Janie thought, turning her head away from him. "He doesn't know how I feel." She closed her eyes.

"I'll be back later," he said with a smile as he left the room. "We can talk more then."

"Fat chance!" Janie thought angrily.

A moment later she heard a soft tap on the door.

"Oh, no! Not again!" Janie whined, thinking that the doctor had returned.

"I'm here to clean your room."

She opened her eyes and saw a man ...an older man dressed in hospital work clothes standing at the foot of her bed.

"Fine!" she responded acidly.

"I hope you will feel better soon," he said sincerely.

"Of all the nerve!" she thought. "I don't want to talk to him."

The man remained at the end of the bed, staring at Janie. The way he looked at her made Janie very uncomfortable and she wanted him out of her room.

"Get the cleaning done and get out!" she ordered. "I want to be by myself."

"All right," he replied softly, then turned and left the room.

Janie stared at the door as he closed it quietly. She had a strange feeling about the man ... a feeling she didn't understand. It was like she knew him but couldn't remember how. She puzzled over this for a few minutes and then let it go.

CHAPTER THIRTEEN

*F*or days Janie continued to speak unkindly to everyone around her and to feel sorry for herself much of the time.

Rose had not mentioned the hiking stick to Janie when Emily brought it to the hospital. Her hope was that Janie would notice it standing against the wall directly across from the foot of her bed and mention it, but she had ignored its presence until today.

Rose, Hunter and Emily were sitting quietly by Janie's bed while she slept. When Janie awoke she opened her eyes and looked directly at the hiking stick. She slowly raised her head off the pillow, squinted her eyes, and looked at it.

"How did that thing get here?" she muttered to herself.

Rose stood and went to Janie's bed smiling, glad that her granddaughter had finally acknowledged the hiking stick being in her room.

"I asked Emily to bring it," Rose said, smiling at Janie.

"Why? I'm not going to hike anywhere with this leg," Janie said, motioning to her broken leg.

"I'll tell you why it's here," Rose said, putting her hand on Janie's shoulder. "Do you remember when I gave you the stick on your wedding day?"

Janie didn't respond.

"And I told you about its history?"

Janie remained silent.

"No? Well, I'm going to refresh your memory," Rose said.

"I'm not interested," Janie snapped at her grandmother.

"Now, you listen to me, Janie," Rose said firmly. "I had this stick brought here to remind you of the women in our family who have owned it. They overcame life threatening experiences and survived. Each time you look at it I want you to remember their strengths. You are a Cherokee woman. I want you to be strong and overcome what has happened in your life."

Janie stared at the stick while her grandmother talked, but still did not respond.

"Janie, will you try to do that?" Rose asked kindly, putting her arm around the stiff shoulders of her granddaughter.

Janie didn't answer.

"Janie?"

Janie nodded slightly, but remained silent.

"Hunter, Emily and I are going downstairs to get something to eat," Rose said. "We'll be back shortly," Rose added as she left Janie's bedside.

When the three reached the door to leave Rose glanced back at Janie. She saw that Janie was staring at the hiking stick. She nodded with a smile and then eased the door closed as they left the room.

As Janie continued to stare at the hiking stick, her thoughts flew back to the many stories her grandmother had shared with her about the courage of her Cherokee ancestors. Like in a dream Janie traveled back in time and shivered, thinking about the harsh cold her Great Great Grandmother White Feather, had endured while traveling the Trail of Tears. She remembered that Grandmother Rose had told her how White Feather had survived. Her thoughts moved on to her Grandmother Rose remembering that she had been kidnapped and how she overcame that terrible time in her life. As these thoughts raced through Janie's mind her body started to relax and a sense of peace began to replace the turmoil she had felt since learning of the death of her beloved husband and unborn child. She wondered also if she could overcome this tragedy. Did she have the strength of her Cherokee ancestors?

CHAPTER FOURTEEN

*R*ose had hoped that the presence of the hiking stick would bring a renewed strength to Janie's mind and a peace to her spirit. It did seem to help for a while, but Janie's mood swings continued and at times even grew worse. Everyone was concerned for her state of mind and her inability to cope with her loss. Nothing seemed to help.

After days of Janie's continual verbal abuse directed at her family and the hospital staff, Doctor Tremont asked the family to come to his office.

"I think it would be a good idea if all of you left the hospital for a few days," he began when all were seated.

"What?" Rose asked, surprised at his request.

"I think all of you need to go home for a few days and leave Janie by herself," he said firmly.

"But, doctor, we don't want her to be alone," Emily said.

"She won't be alone. We must give her time to work through this anger by herself."

Rose shook her head sadly from side to side.

"Her behavior is normal," Doctor Tremont said kindly. "The anger Janie's showing is the result of the deep hurt she's experiencing. She is working herself back to the reality of what has happened."

"But..." Hunter began.

"Trust me, it will help her," Doctor Tremont interrupted. "All of you need to rest."

"I suppose you are right," Rose said slowly.

"Soon Doctor Wade will perform the plastic surgery on her face."

"Plastic surgery?" asked Emily, surprised.

Doctor Tremont nodded.

"No one has told us about plastic surgery," Hunter said.

"Does Janie know?" Rose asked.

"Yes", Doctor Tremont smiled. "Janie knows."

"And does she want the surgery?" Rose asked.

"Well, yes and no," he chuckled. "She says that she doesn't care one way or the other, but, of course, before the surgery is performed she will be required to give a written request stating her permission for the operation.   The final decision will be hers after she talks with the surgeon."

"Is it a safe procedure?" Rose asked.

"Yes... and the recuperation period is fairly short," Doctor Tremont said. "She will have one of the best plastic surgeons in the United States. His work is highly respected in the medical community. He is in demand constantly and we are fortunate to have him on our hospital staff."

"And the surgery is absolutely necessary, doctor?" Rose asked.

"Janie's face is scarred from all the glass cuts she received in the accident, but after Dr. Wade performs the surgery no one will ever know about the facial scars."

"But...doctor..." Hunter said, but the doctor did not let him finish.

"She will be well cared for here in our hospital," Doctor Tremont smiled. "By the way, all of you have met Nurse Millie, haven't you?"

"Yes, indeed," Rose said, glancing at Hunter with a slight smile.

"We are all acquainted with her," Hunter said. "She has been very good to Janie...and us."

The doctor nodded. "Millie has become a good friend to Janie and has told me that she will be spending time with her...even when she is not working. They have gotten to know each other quite well. Millie will keep a close eye on her."

Doctor Tremont stood and moved to the door and opened it. "Now, all of you go home and rest for a while. Janie will be in good hands."

"Thank you, doctor," Rose said. "We appreciate all that you have done for her."

While Emily and Hunter visited Janie to tell her they were going home for a while Rose sat down in the waiting room and called Tara.

"Tara, I'm coming home for a few days...in fact, we are all going home."

"Oh, is Janie better?"

"Well, physically-yes, but emotionally –no. We're leaving by doctor's orders. Can you come and pick me up? We'll talk more on the drive home."

"Sure. When do you want me to come?"

"I'll be ready whenever you can make it."

"I'm not doing anything today. I can come now."

"Good."

"I'll see you soon."

"Thank you. Tara. Please be careful."

Before Rose left the hospital she went to Janie's room.

"I'm going home for a few days, Janie, now that you're feeling better," she said after hugging her granddaughter.

"I'm not better," Janie snapped at her grandmother. "I won't ever be better."

Rose gently pushed a strand of hair away from Janie's face. "Yes, honey, you will," Rose said.

"No! I won't!" Janie hissed, not looking at her grandmother.

Rose smiled. "As soon as all the cuts on your face heal a plastic surgeon will be in to see you and discuss an operation."

"Well, I've decided that I don't want anything done to my face," Janie said, raising her voice. "I don't care if I stay scarred for the rest of my life. What do I care?"

Rose leaned over to her granddaughter and hugged her again.

"I'll see you soon," she whispered.

Janie turned her head away from her grandmother.

Rose shook her head, gathered her belongings and

walked to the foot of the bed.

"I love you, Janie. I'll call you soon."

"Don't bother," Janie muttered under her breath.

Rose shook her head sadly and slipped quietly out of the room, tears now running down her face for the granddaughter she loved so much.

When the door closed Janie looked at the hiking stick for a moment. She was confused. She closed her eyes. Every time she looked at the stick she felt a renewed strength, but just as quickly her hurting heart caused her to say mean things. She desperately needed someone to blame for her loss and she also needed to find the strength to face the future and the will to go on with her life. As she gazed at the hiking stick again she prayed for the strength of her ancestors. Then she turned her head and buried her face in the pillow and sobbed loudly.

CHAPTER FIFTEEN

The next day Janie eagerly watched the door of her room each time it opened, secretly hoping to see someone in the family. But she saw only members of the hospital staff. And where was Millie she wondered? She had not been in to see her either.

The following day was the same. By the end of the third day Janie was beginning to become lonely and miss her family and Millie.

The man who came to clean her room always tried to engage her in conversation, but she would turn her head away and ignore him. He made Janie nervous and uneasy, especially when she noticed him staring at her. After days of concern she was considering asking one of the nurses to have him replaced.

However, something happened one day that sparked Janie's interest while she watched him out of the corner of her eye.

When he leaned over to pick up the trash basket she saw something blue flip out from under the neck of his shirt. He quickly pushed it back in its hiding place and glanced toward Janie to see if she had noticed.

Janie thought that it had looked like a large blue turquoise stone...and for some reason she was very attracted to it.

"I wonder where he got that nugget," she pondered. "I know a lot of people in this area wear turquoise jewelry so that's not unusual, I suppose." Still she was strongly drawn to the beautiful nugget she had glimpsed.

The next day when he returned to her room Janie watched him more closely when he was not looking at her. She hoped to get another look at the stone but it was apparent that he was concentrating on keeping it hidden under his shirt.

For the next few days when he returned to Janie's room she continued trying to catch a glimpse of the nugget, but failed. Her curiosity about the nugget was beginning to replace her fear of the man. Now she looked forward every day to his coming to her room to clean.

Late one afternoon Millie arrived, pushing the door open with her usual gusto.

"Hello, my friend," she chirped, walking to Janie's bed. "Did you miss me?"

"No!" Janie replied sharply.

"Yes, you did. I can tell." Millie laughed and bounced up on the bed beside Janie.

"Millie, there's something I want to ask you," Janie began when Millie was settled.

"Okay. What is it?" Millie responded, glad her new friend was showing an interest in something.

"What do you know about the man who cleans my room?"

"What?" Millie asked, turning to look directly at Janie in surprise.

"What do you know about him?"

"The cleaning man?"

"Yes."

"Why?"

"He makes me feel uncomfortable. I catch him staring at me every time he's in my room."

"Oh, he's probably harmless, honey. Don't worry about him," Millie replied, patting Janie on the hand. "I imagine he's just looking at all those bandages on your face and wondering what you look like under them."

"I don't know," Janie said slowly.

"He's okay."

"What do you know about him?" Janie asked again, pushing for an answer.

"Not much, really. He began working here recently, actually, a few days after you were admitted. He's very polite and does his job well, but I'm afraid that he's going to be fired."

"Fired?"

Millie nodded her head.

"Why?"

"He's absent from work a lot. He says it's due to illness. Why do you want to know about him?"

"I don't know, Millie...there's just something about him," Janie said slowly. "I can't put my finger on it."

"Well," Millie said, sliding off the bed, "don't worry. He's trying to earn a living. He's very kind. He's a good worker and everyone on the staff seems to like him."

Despite Millie's words Janie still had a strange feeling every time she saw the cleaning man even though much of her fear had been replaced by curiosity. She hoped he wouldn't be fired and she also wondered about his illness.

CHAPTER SIXTEEN

As soon as the cleaning man entered Janie's room the next day she pushed herself up to a sitting position and watched him carefully. She tried to see the nugget when he came near her, but could only see the outline of it under his shirt. She felt that it was obvious he was trying to hide it from her. But why?

When he moved closer to Janie's bed to pick up the trash basket she glanced at his hand covered with a rubber glove. She stared at his hand and thought she saw something blue under the glove.

"Are you wearing a turquoise ring?" she asked bravely.

"What?" he asked surprised, pausing to look at Janie.

"Are you wearing a turquoise ring?" she repeated.

He took a step away from Janie and put the hand wearing the ring into his pocket, then resumed cleaning the room without answering Janie.

"I love turquoise. I'd like to see your ring and the nugget you wear," Janie said.

His hand flew to cover the nugget imprint against his shirt. He backed away from Janie and turned to leave the room.

"Wait! Please," Janie called to him as he put his hand on the door handle. "I know that you are wearing turquoise. I love the stone. Please, may I see your nugget and ring?"

He shook his head, refusing Janie's request.

"Please," she begged.

Slowly he walked back to the edge of Janie's bed and withdrew his hand from his pocket and slipped off the glove, his eyes never leaving Janie. He leaned over slightly and extended his hand toward her.

She took his hand and brought it close to her face.

"It's beautiful," Janie whispered.

The silver ring held three rectangular turquoise stones set in it and Janie had a strange feeling that she had seen the ring before.

"I'm being silly," she thought. "I've seen many turquoise rings in the gallery. I've probably seen one similar to this one."

"Would you let me see the nugget you wear around your neck?"

Without answering he withdrew the nugget from under his shirt and leaned over so Janie could get a better look.

"I love it," she said, smiling.

"I must go now," he said and abruptly left the room, leaving Janie wondering why she was so attracted to the two pieces of jewelry he wore.

That night Janie had been asleep about two hours when she was suddenly awakened by a disturbing dream. She sat up and put her hand to her chest. Her heart was pounding wildly. She looked into the dimness of the room for a moment and then eased herself back down on the bed and thought about the dream.

In her dream she was a little child again, sitting on her Daddy's lap, playing with the turquoise stone he wore on a chain around his neck. Then she was wearing the turquoise ring that belonged to her Daddy. She twirled it around and around on her finger and laughed. She loved playing with the jewelry.

She couldn't remember when she last had thought of her father. He had disappeared when she was very young and her mother never liked to talk about him. Janie remembered that he was a tall man who had laughed a lot. He would get on the floor and ride her on his back while she wore his big ring. She could never understand why he had gone away and she had cried herself to sleep many nights after they returned home without him. The house was lonely without him and her mother had to work hard to support her family. Not knowing what happened to him had left so many unanswered questions and now this man had brought all those past memories to the surface again.

Janie lay awake for a long time, finally closing her eyes and begging sleep to come once more.

Dawn came but the bright morning sun could not dispel Janie's unsettled feelings. Maybe she would see him again today...and finally she nodded off to sleep.

CHAPTER SEVENTEEN

"Wake up, Janie!" Millie said urgently, shaking Janie's shoulder. Then she quickly walked to the window and opened the blinds to allow the sunlight to filter into the room.

"What?" Janie asked, slowly opening her eyes. Her hand traveled up to shade them from the bright light.

"I'm so glad you finally agreed to have plastic surgery on your face," Millie said, smiling at Janie.

"Uh-huh," Janie responded half asleep.

"Wake up, Janie," Millie urged, shaking her shoulder again. "Have you met your plastic surgeon yet?"

"No," Janie said, yawning.

"Well, he's on his way to see you," Millie smiled.

"So?"

"So, sit up, girl," Millie said, pushing Janie's beautiful black hair back from her face.

"Why?" Janie asked, moving Millie's hand away from her face.

Millie rolled her eyes at Janie and threw up her arms.

"Brush your hair," she ordered, thrusting a brush in Janie's hand.

"Why?" Janie asked again.

"Because he's beautiful!" Millie gushed.

"Oh, Millie," Janie said, turning her head on the pillow and closing her eyes.

"Janie! Wake up!" Millie demanded, shaking her again.

A brisk knock on the door echoed through the room and it opened quickly.

"Good morning, I'm Doctor Wade, your plastic surgeon," he said, walking to Janie's bed. "How are you this morning?"

Janie did not respond.

"And you're Janie," he said, looking at the medical chart he held in his hands.

"Yes," Janie replied quietly, slowly turning over in the bed and looking up.

Doctor Wade moved closer to the bed. "Would you sit up for me, please?"

Janie pulled herself up to a sitting position.

Only a few bandages remained on Janie's face and the doctor removed them carefully. "I want to look at these scars before we begin removing them," he said, tracing over the scars with his fingertips.

Millie stood behind the doctor, looking at Janie.

When Janie glanced over at her Millie winked, nodded toward the doctor and gave Janie a thumbs up signal.

"I'll be in to see you before the surgery to discuss the procedure and answer any questions you might have," he said, making notes on Janie's medical chart. Then he turned to leave.

He stopped and glanced at the hiking stick on his way out of the room.

"Beautiful," he said to Janie, nodding at the stick and then he was gone.

Millie immediately rushed to Janie's bedside the moment the doctor disappeared from the room.

"Isn't he handsome?" Millie sighed.

"Uh-huh." Janie responded indifferently.

"Listen, I've got to run. I'm on duty, but I'll be back as soon as my shift ends," Millie said before leaving the room.

Janie thought about the man who would operate on her face and she had to agree with Millie.

He was one of the most handsome young men she had ever seen. He was tall with wide shoulders and had dark eyes...beautiful eyes like pools of black ink. His black straight hair was so dark that it looked like a deep blue color, much like her own hair.

Janie was tired from lack of sleep the night before and she closed her eyes to take a nap. She was almost asleep when Millie rushed back into the room.

"Isn't he gorgeous?" Millie gushed like a schoolgirl. "And did you see that smile?"

"Yes." Janie responded.

"That smile could melt an iceberg!" Millie said, rolling her eyes upward.

"Millie, haven't you ever seen him before?"

"Yes, but not often. He travels to hospitals all over the United States."

"Really?"

"Yes," she grinned.

Janie did not respond.

"Around here some of the nurses think he's a snob, but I think he's just shy around women."

Janie smiled, amazed at her new friend.

Millie glanced at her watch. "Got to run back to work... I'll see you later."

Janie smiled again as she watched her friend leave the room and decided that Millie definitely had a crush on the doctor.

The door burst open half way and Millie's head appeared around the small opening. "I'm glad to see that you are smiling again!" she said.

This made Janie chuckle out loud and the sound of her own laughter startled her, realizing that it was the first time she had laughed since the accident.

"Well, maybe I'll get through this after all," she thought, "but where is my family?"

Janie wanted to see her brother and sister and definitely her grandmother.

"I miss them," she whispered.

CHAPTER EIGHTEEN

$\mathcal{S}$everal days passed and Janie was disappointed that the cleaning man had not returned to her room. She was anxious to see the nugget and the ring again. Each time the door to her room opened she hoped it would be him. The dream she had experienced helped her to remember the necklace and ring that her Daddy had worn. Now she was anxious to talk to him again to see if he would tell her where he had gotten the jewelry.

When he finally returned to Janie's room he wore a high neck shirt and kept his distance from her bed. It was obvious that he was concealing his hand wearing the ring.

Janie's eyes followed his every move and waited for him to speak, but he went about his work silently ignoring her presence.

"Where did you get the turquoise ring?" Janie blurted out, breaking the silence between them.

"What?" he asked, pausing to look at Janie.

"The ring...where did you get it?" Janie said, motioning to his hand.

"I've had it for a long, long time," he said, evading her question, turning his back to Janie. He remained silent and did not look at her.

"Would you let me hold it?"

Not responding, he continued working.

"Please," Janie said, sitting up in bed, "may I see it, please?"

The man looked at her, then nodded slowly and reluctantly slipped off the glove and removed the ring from his finger. He walked to Janie's bed and handed it to her.

Janie took the ring and turned it over and over in her hand, looking at every detail of the silver carved designs and turquoise stones.

"My father had a ring like this one," she said quietly, more to herself than to the man. "I remember the design of his ring."

The man stood silently by Janie's bed, watching her every move.

"He told me that it was one of a kind," Janie said, staring at the ring.

The man nodded and looked down.

Janie stared at him. "He's dead and I don't know what happened to the ring," she said.

Slowly the man's eyes locked with Janie's eyes. "No," he said softly, "he's not dead."

"What?"

"Your Daddy's not dead," he repeated, continuing to look into her eyes.

"Yes, he is," Janie insisted.

"No," the man said, moving his head from side to side.

"How do you know?" Janie asked, searching the man's face for an answer.

Slowly the man withdrew the turquoise nugget necklace from under his shirt. He slipped the chain off over his head and extended it toward Janie.

"Look," he said.

"Come closer," Janie said. She reached out and touched the nugget. Memories of her childhood and her Daddy flooded over her. She looked up and gazed into the man's face.

"Who are you?" she asked in a hoarse whisper.

As tears formed in his eyes he hesitated and then spoke.

"I'm your Daddy, Janie," he stammered, his voice breaking.

"No! My Daddy is dead!"

"I am your Daddy, Janie."

Janie gasped. "NO!" She shook her head from side to side, tears forming in her eyes.

"Yes." he repeated quietly, nodding his head.

Janie stared at the nugget and the ring she held in her hand. They seemed familiar to her, but still she didn't believe that this stranger could be her Daddy.

"Maybe this man stole the jewelry from my Daddy. Maybe Daddy sold the ring and nugget to him. Maybe...." Questions raced through her mind.

Janie took a deep breath as she looked at the stranger in front of her.

"What is your name?" she demanded.

"Don," he said softly.

Janie looked down for a moment and then back at the man's face.

"Tell me where you and my mother met."

"Oklahoma...at an Indian Pow Wow," he answered quickly, taking a handkerchief from his pocket and wiping his tears.

Janie stared at him, thunderstruck. She had heard her mother tell the story of their meeting many times, but her Daddy could have also told this man the story. Her doubts continued despite the deep emotion that this man was showing. Could he really be her Daddy? Could he really be alive?

The man standing before her didn't look anything like the Daddy she remembered. This man was thin and stooped. He was almost bald and his wispy hair was a dingy white. His skin was wrinkled and pasty looking. He couldn't be the vibrant, handsome man she had held in her memory, but how did he get her father's jewelry.

"You are my daughter," he said, looking directly at Janie.

"No!"

"When you were a little girl you always loved my jewelry. You would climb up into my lap and play with the nugget and the ring," he said, reflecting on the past, hoping that he could convince Janie that she was his daughter.

Janie did not respond. She sat staring at the nugget and ring in her hands. Then she raised her head and glared at the man as sudden anger rose in her voice.

"If you are my Daddy..." she said bitterly "...you left us!!"

"Yes, I did," he admitted, hanging his head.

His hands began to tremble.

"You left us at the camp alone,,,"

"Yes," he interrupted.

"...while the searchers tried to find you."

The accusation in Janie's voice was like a knife stabbing in his heart.

"I'm sorry. I..."

"We thought you were dead!" Janie interrupted. She stared into his face.

But Janie's thoughts were also trying to accept the reality that this man could actually be her father. Finally, awe stricken and with tears in her eyes, she realized that the man was telling the truth. This was the lost father they had mourned...the man they had loved and had lost. She stared at him. Her emotions were like a whirlwind. With the realization that he was telling her the truth other memories sprang into her mind...how the men had searched for him, how much the family had missed him, how hard their mother had worked to support them, how she had cried in the night when she thought her brother and sister would not hear. All these things came rushing back like an avalanche tumbling helter-skelter through her mind. And suddenly ...anger! Anger so fierce it was like a visible force moving straight at him.

She could see he needed to explain. He moved closer to the bed and began. "I was young and foolish...and a coward who didn't want the responsibility of a family. I loved Ruth and you children, but..." he began, his voice croaking and muffled.

"Enough to leave us!" Janie spit out at him.

"I loved..." he began again.

"NO!" Janie interrupted, her voice rising. "You didn't love us or you wouldn't have abandoned us!"

"Regardless of what you think, Janie, I loved your mother and you kids. I was a young irresponsible man who couldn't take the pressure of providing for a family."

"You..."

"Please, let me finish, Janie," he said, raising a shaking hand. "I have anguished over what I did to my family every day of my life since I left. I beg that Ruth and you kids will forgive me...please."

Janie snapped her head around to stare at him through her tears.

"Mother died!" she yelled out at him.

"She is dead?" he asked softly, disbelief and anguish sounding in his voice.

"Yes" Janie screamed again at him.

Dropping his head he covered his eyes with shaking hands while the tears rolled down his cheeks.

"I'm so sorry," he whispered, looking at Janie. "I loved her."

"Yeah! Right!" Janie said angrily.

"I loved Ruth and you children and...."

"Enough to leave us?"

"Please believe me."

Their eyes met.

His eyes were filled with remorse begging for forgiveness, hoping she would understand.

"Get out of my room!" Janie snarled at the man standing near her and rose to a sitting position. She pointed to the door. "GET OUT!"

"Janie...let me ex..."

"I said, GET OUT!" she yelled, flinging the ring and necklace at him.

The jewelry bounced off his chest and onto the floor. Slowly he bent over and picked up the ring and necklace and moved to the door. He paused, then turned back and looked at Janie.

"I'm sorry," he said, "so sorry."

He hung his head, shoulders sagging and slipped quietly out of the room, passing Millie as she entered.

Millie rushed to Janie's bedside. She knew something had upset her friend terribly and she was ready to take up the fray. She was even more concerned when Janie suddenly buried her face in her hands and sobbed uncontrollable.

"Janie, what's the matter?" Millie asked. "Janie..."

Janie didn't answer as Millie leaned over and looked closely at her.

"What happened? Did the cleaning man hurt you?"

Janie shook her head from side to side while Millie gathered her friend into her arms.

"Maybe this is what she needed," Millie thought. "My mother always said a good cry was better medicine than a ton of pills."

She held Janie close and rocked her back and forth like a precious baby.

And ...she prayed that her mother was right.

Janie's thoughts were filled with so many pent-up feelings. This man had just turned her already destroyed life into an emotional turmoil. She was being torn between joy and anger, remembering love and then instant hate. How could she cope with this new upheaval in her life? Where was her family? She needed Grandmother Rose! She needed...

Suddenly, as she was shaking her head in denial, over Millie's shoulder she glimpsed the hicking stick standing like a sentinel in the corner of the room. She knew she could be a strong Cherokee woman! And with this thought she felt warmth come over her like she was being enfolded in soft downy wings.

CHAPTER NINETEEN

*D*uring the next few days Janie was very quiet and glad that her family was not visiting her...or Millie who was off duty. She wasn't ready to share the experience of meeting her Daddy with any of them. She needed time to be alone and think about what had happened.

Janie had not seen Don since the day they had spoke...and she did not want to see him again, but after a few days when Millie returned to work, she mentioned his absence to her friend.

"Millie, what happened to the man who cleaned my room?" Janie asked, trying to sound unconcerned. "He hasn't been in lately. I have a new cleaning lady."

"Oh, honey, didn't you hear?"

"Hear what?"

"Don died."

"He died?" Janie asked softly.

"Yes. He had cancer."

"How do you know, Millie?"

"One of the nurses told me. She said that he knew he didn't have long to live when he came here to work. She thought it was unusual that he wanted to work instead of staying home and taking it easy," Millie said, hustling around the bed straightening the sheets. And she wondered why Janie was interested in him after she had not wanted him around.

A few days later Millie burst into Janie's room carrying a small box.

"Janie! Look! This came to the hospital for you this morning," she said, extending the box toward Janie.

Janie raised herself up in the bed. "What?"

"This is for you," Millie repeated. "Someone sent you a present."

"Who's it from?"

"I don't know," Millie said, turning the box over, searching for the identification of the sender. "There's no name on it. Here," Millie thrust the box into Janie's hand.

"Who would send me a present?"

"Open it," Millie said, excited to see what was in the package.

"What do you suppose it is?" Janie asked, looking at the small box.

"I don't know that either...so will you please open it?" Millie said, climbing up on the bed to sit by Janie.

Slowly Janie peeled away the paper on the box. When she lifted the lid off she gasped and her hands began to tremble. Her eyes widened in disbelief.

"What's wrong, Janie?"

Janie shook her head slowly as she stared into the box. Nestled inside it lay the turquoise ring, the nugget necklace and a folded piece of paper. With shaking hands Janie slowly took the paper out of the box and unfolded it.

"Do you want me to leave, Janie?" Millie asked softly, wondering if Janie needed privacy.

"No, don't go," Janie answered, taking Millie's hand. "Stay with me, please."

Millie slid off the bed and pulled a chair close. She folded her hands in her lap and looked at Janie.

"It's a letter," Janie said, glanced at her friend and nodded. She took a deep breath and continued.

"Janie, my darling daughter,"

Millie looked up at Janie in surprise, but said nothing.

Janie glanced at her friend, then back to the letter. She nodded, took a deep breathe and began reading.

"I'm not able to go to work at the hospital anymore. I am not feeling well. Today I will spend some time writing this note and putting the ring and nugget in the

box for you.

I want you to know the truth about what happened after my cowardly departure from my family many years ago at the campsite.

I had planned to return, but when I went deeper into the woods I kept running. It started raining...I was in the rain for a day and a half before I finally found a small cave high in the mountains to give me shelter. It was very small. I couldn't stand up in it, but was glad to have protection from the rain. I had eaten all the food I had brought with me. I was very hungry. I was ashamed to return to the camp so I kept walking. I found berries and water in the woods and I lived on them for another day. I kept walking and finally reached Gatlinburg. By that time I had grown a beard. I was glad because I felt that it would be hard for anyone to recognize me.

I had a little money so I bought food and a few clothes and headed north catching rides when I could. I worked at various jobs while I traveled and eventually I ended up in Canada. I was able to get a job and I stayed there for a few years. Always my plan was to make enough money to come back and ask my family for forgiveness. When I made my way back down south I became ill but I kept going.

When I got to Kentucky I saw an article in a newspaper about the terrible automobile accident and saw your name. I read that you were in the hospital in Ashville. I wasn't sure that you would want to see me, but I knew I had to be with you while you recovered and I hoped to see Ruth and the other children at the hospital too."

Janie stopped reading and wiped the tears from her eyes with her fingertips, then looked at her friend. Millie handed Janie a tissue, but said nothing. Her eyes were filled with tears also.

Millie stared at Janie, their eyes locking for a moment before Janie looked down and began reading again.

"Regardless of what you think, Janie, I loved my wife and my children. I was wrong to leave all of you.

I have anguished over it every day of my life.

I'm not feeling well today. I have spent the day writing this note and cleaning the nugget and ring for you. I have made arrangements for them to be delivered to you after my death.

I will die a poor man. The nugget and ring are all I have to give you...my first born. I know you loved them. I want you to have the only possessions I own. I hope that they will bring happy memories back to you when you look at them and remember the happy times we shared together.

Again, forgive me...please. Gv ge yu (I love you)
                                   Until we meet again,
                                      Your Dad."

Millie had not taken her eyes off Janie while she read the letter. She was shocked at its contents and occasionally wiped tears from her own face.

When Janie finished reading the letter she slowly folded it and put it back in the box. Then she took the jewelry out of the box and put the turquoise necklace around her neck and slipped the ring on her finger while silent tears cascaded down her face.

"Millie, I..." Janie halted. Words failed her. All she could do was look at Millie with tears flowing.

"Oh, Janie," Millie whispered as she stood and went to her friend, arms outstretched. She gathered Janie into her arms and held her close until the sobs became hiccups and finally ended.

Janie thought about the many tears she had shed since being in the hospital. She felt drained and exhausted, but strangely she felt release.

"Maybe," she thought, "my tears are the healing power Millie's mother believes in and the strengthening my hiking stick symbolizes.

As thoughts crossed Janie's mind she felt a flutter of hope and again a warm sensation around her shoulders as if she had been hugged by an angel.

Later Millie walked out of Janie's room as she thought of everything that had recently happened to this young woman who had become her patient and was now her new friend. She wondered if Janie had the strength to overcome these things and go on with her life. Her grandmother believed it was possible. The thought of Janie's Grandmother Rose reminded Millie of the mystery of the beautiful hiking stick that stood in the corner of Janie's room. One day she would ask her friend to tell her about it.

CHAPTER TWENTY

$\mathcal{A}$ week had passed since the arrival of Don's letter and jewelry and Janie was struggling with bouts of depression. She read the letter over and over and mourned yet another loss.

"What has happened to my life?" she wondered while her thoughts raced on. "I was so happy and suddenly everything changed. First, my husband and baby were lost and then my pet Wa-Yah. Even my father who I lost so many years ago reappeared only to be taken away from me."

"And now," she whispered softly, "even my family has deserted me. I am so alone." She felt that she had no one to lean on, no one to make all the bad things go away.

Millie had tried to cheer her up, but had failed.

Rose had been told about Don and she had wanted to return to the hospital earlier but Dr. Tremont had wanted to see how Janie coped with this on her own. Now he had called Rose to return to the hospital, thinking that her presence would help Janie.

"She's having more good days now than bad; however, we want to try to lift her spirits before the plastic surgery. She's not angry like she was before, but she's depressed again. Her surgery has been scheduled and Doctor Wade will be in to speak to her in the next few days. I would like for you to be present then, if possible."

""Yes, of course, doctor. I'll come tomorrow," Rose had agreed.

Millie bounced into Janie's room with a big grin on her face.

"Hey! How are you doing today?"

Before Janie could reply Millie spied the hiking stick. She picked it up and turned it over and over in her hands. "I've wanted to ask you about this," she said.

Janie remained silent

"It's very pretty. Is it new?"

"No. Actually it's very old. It's been in our family for a long time."

"It's beautiful," Millie said, running her fingers up and down the stick.

"Grandmother gave it to me on my wedding day."

"Really?"

"Yes."

"Will you tell me about the stick sometime?" Millie asked, running her hands over the intricate carvings. "I'm on duty now, but I'll be back soon."

Janie nodded.

The next day Rose returned to the hospital and Janie was very glad to see her. They hugged each other for a long time and Janie began to apologize for her behavior, but Rose kissed her and assured Janie all was well between them.

Janie was relieved to have her grandmother with her again. She immediately began to tell her everything at once with her words tumbling out of her mouth.

Rose held up both hands, smiled and exclaimed. "Wait just a minute!"

She put her things away and pulled a chair close to Janie's bed. "Now," she said, "Tell me everything."

Janie told her grandmother about the plastic surgeon and they laughed when she told her about Millie having a crush on the handsome young doctor who would perform the operation.

"Is he as handsome as you say?" Rose asked Janie with a smile.

"Oh, yes," replied Janie with a smile.

Janie told her grandmother about Don visiting her when he worked at the hospital and showed her the ring and turquoise necklace...and the letter.

Rose did not comment, but her eyes betrayed her

feelings. She was visibly surprised and shocked but she told Janie that she would reserve her comments until later.

"I need to think about this for a while," Rose said.

Janie had become sad as she told Rose about Don and seemed very tired. She had finally drifted off into a restless sleep thinking about her father as her grandmother sat nearby.

Later that day Millie entered the room cheerful, as usual.

"Miss Rose! I'm glad to see you." Millie said, and gave Rose an affectionate hug.

She turned to Janie. "I thought I'd come in and see my favorite patient before I started my shift," she said, walking to Janie's bed.

Janie didn't respond, but did manage a slight smile.

"Why don't you go relax a bit, Miss Rose, and maybe have something to eat? I'll be here with Janie for a little while," offered Millie.

"I believe I will, Millie, while you're here to keep Janie company."

When Rose passed Millie on her way out she whispered. "She seems to be a little low today. See if you can help her."

Millie nodded.

"How are you feeling today?"

Janie didn't respond.

"Are you not talking today?" Millie asked good naturally.

"I'm hurting, Millie," Janie said sarcastically.

"Do you need medication for the pain?"

"It's not that kind of pain, Millie...it's about finding out about my Daddy...my Daddy that I thought was dead."

"All right," Millie said, straightening the bed covers. "Do you want to talk about it?"

"And you don't know how your heart hurts when you lose your baby and husband."

"Well, no, not a baby, but I sure know what it feels like to lose an almost-husband," Millie said.

"An almost-husband?" Janie looked at Millie quickly.

Millie nodded her head.

"Yep! That's right."

"Were you married, Millie?" Janie asked, her curiosity growing.

"Like I said...almost," Millie answered.

"What happened?" Janie asked. She sat up as Millie stood and pushed another pillow behind her back.

"Well," Millie said, pulling a chair close to the bed, and then sitting down, "on the night before our wedding we had our wedding rehearsal. I was inside the church taking care of all the last minute details. When I finished I didn't see my husband-to be anywhere."

"Did he leave, Millie?" Janie interrupted, struggling to pull herself up to a sitting position in the bed and becoming more interested.

"Oh, no, I found him...found him out in the parking lot in his car with my maid-of-honor," Millie answered, looking down at her hands clasped tightly in her lap.

"Millie!" exclaimed Janie, catching her breath. "How awful!"

"Yep! There they were in the back seat...and they weren't discussing the wedding...in fact, they weren't talking at all."

"Oh, Millie! That's terrible!"

"It hurt for a long, long time," Millie remembered.

Janie nodded, tears forming in her eyes.

"People never knew why I called off the wedding," Millie whispered softly, looking up at Janie.

Silence filled the room.

A few moments later Millie continued. "Nope! I never told anyone why the wedding was cancelled at the last minute."

"Why not, Millie?"

Millie shrugged. "Oh, I don't know. I was too hurt to explain, I suppose."

Janie shook her head slowly. "What did you do?"

"I left town...went to Myrtle Beach for a couple of weeks and licked my wounds," she smiled sadly.

Janie's gaze swept over Millie, her feisty, happy little nurse. She was always smiling. She couldn't imagine the deep hurt Millie must have endured under all the smiles.

"What happened to him, Millie?" Janie asked softly.

"The last news I heard was that he had moved to Maryland."

Janie nodded.

"And I hope he stays there!" Millie laughed softly, pushing herself up from the chair.

"Come here," Janie motioned to her new friend.

Janie reached up and pulled Millie close and hugged her.

"I'm so sorry, Millie," said Janie.

At that moment Janie realized that there are all kinds of hurt in life and she was not the only one to have suffered one of them. She knew that there was a bond now between her and her new friend...a bond that would not be severed. Both had suffered tremendous hurt in their young lives...and both understood deep pain.

"Thank you," Millie whispered.

Janie glanced over Millie's shoulder with misty eyes and stared at the hiking stick leaning against the wall. Her grandmother's words flooded over her.

"Grandmother, the whining and crying are over," she whispered. "From now on I will be a strong woman...a strong Cherokee woman like those women who have come before me. I will survive and find happiness in my life again."

CHAPTER TWENTY-ONE

*T*he plastic surgery was over and Janie was recuperating much faster than expected. Also her disposition had improved... to the relief of everyone.

Rose, Hunter and Emily had spaced their visits to come once a week and Janie had finally told her sister and brother about Don and had shown them the ring and nugget. They were too young to recall any memories of their Daddy or the jewelry and their reactions had been mixed with anger and tears.

"Do you want to see an old friend?' a voice rang out from behind the half-opened door.

"Tara!" Janie called, immediately recognizing the voice. "Come in!"

Tara rushed to the bed with open arms and the two women embraced.

"Well, I know that you're not going to run in the marathon this year, but I did find out that you are going to have a new face," Tara teased, tapping the bandages lightly on Janie's face.

"Nope! Won't race this year. I'm still in rehab for this leg..."Janie laughed, "...and I don't know what I'll look like when all these bandages come off."

"Just as beautiful as you were before the accident!" Tara exclaimed, patting Janie on the shoulder.

Both women laughed.

"Tara, you always know how to make me laugh."

"Be a clown – be a clown," Tara sang, dancing around the room, waving her arms in the air.

Janie laughed again.

"Sit down. Tell me all about Steve and yourself. How are the two of you getting along?"

"Good...really good. We're very happy," Tara replied, perching on a chair. "We stay busy...always on the go."

"Well, that's good," remarked Janie. "By the way, when have you seen Grandmother?"

"Yesterday. She's coming to see you in a few days."

"Good."

Tara glanced around the room.

"Just look at all these beautiful flowers!" Tara said, rising and walking to one of the arrangements.

"Yes. I love them," Janie said.

"Who sent this huge bouquet of red roses?" Tara asked, leaning over to smell the flowers.

"I don't know. It didn't have a card with it."

"From a secret admirer, I suppose," Tara laughed, fingering the petals of a large rose.

Janie shook her head. "I doubt that."

"Maybe from your handsome doctor," Tara teased.

"Oh, Tara, he's short, fat and old," Janie laughed again, then added "and probably married."

"I'm not talking about your first doctor. I mean your new one."

"My new one?" Janie asked.

"Yes. The plastic surgeon."

Janie shook her head and smiled. "Oh, him...Doctor Wade?"

"Yes. When did you see him last?" Tara asked, walking to the foot of the bed, and looking at Janie.

"Oh, I don't know," Janie responded indifferently. "Yesterday, I think."

"Trust me, honey. I would remember. He is one of the best looking young men I have ever laid eyes on. I hope he comes in while I'm here," Tara said, looking wishfully toward the door.

"Tara!" Janie laughed.

"He's not married," Tara said, turning back to look at Janie with a twinkle in her eye.

"Now, Tara, how do you know that?" Janie asked.

"I asked!"

"What?" Janie asked again, surprise in her voice.

"I asked Millie," Tara answered, winking at Janie

while nodding her head.

"Tara!"

"Well, I wanted to know and Millie said that he's the most eligible bachelor on the hospital staff."

"Tara, you are something else!" Janie laughed, shaking her head from side to side.

Tara walked to the side of Janie's bed. "Now, when are the bandages coming off?" Tara asked, motioning to Janie's face.

"Soon, I hope," replied Janie.

Janie's supper was brought in and Tara realized she had to get home. She jumped up, gave Janie a quick hug and headed for the door with a wave of her hand.

CHAPTER TWENTY-TWO

*G*ood afternoon, Janie."

Janie awoke with a start, hearing the voice echo through the room. She opened her eyes and squinted at the man standing at the foot of her bed.

"How are you?" Dr. Wade asked pleasantly.

Janie did not reply, instead she stared at the doctor. She noticed that he was not wearing the white coat she was accustomed to seeing.

He wore faded jeans with a white tee shirt and when she glanced down at his feet she noticed that he wore brown scuffed cowboy boots.

"I'm off duty today," he said, coming to her bed. "I've heard that you don't like to venture out of this room. Is that right?"

Janie nodded.

"Well, how about a little ride this afternoon?"

"A ride?"

"Yes," he answered, smiling.

"No. I don't want to get into a car," Janie informed him sternly.

"Not a car ride...at least not yet. I'm talking about a wheelchair ride."

"I don't think so...I'm..."

"I've got a nurse bringing a chair," the doctor interrupted.

"Well, you certainly seem to have made up my mind before asking me," Janie said sarcastically. "I really don't want to leave my bed."

Doctor Wade smiled, a habit Janie would learn to recognize, if not to appreciate.

Suddenly the door swung open and Millie entered pushing a wheelchair and smiling at Janie.

"Here it is, doctor," Millie chirped, pushing the chair close to Janie's bed.

"Thank you, Nurse."

Turning to Janie he smiled. "Sit up, Janie, we're going for a little ride."

"No!" Janie raised her voice.

"Yes! Doctor's orders!" the doctor responded. He pulled back the bed covers, reached under Janie, lifted her easily out of the bed and settled her in the wheelchair.

Millie snickered behind her hand watching the scene taking place before her.

"Thank you, Nurse," the doctor said, looking at Millie. "I won't need you anymore."

When Millie reached the door she looked back and smiled at Janie. Then she gave her a thumbs-up signal of approval.

Janie tossed her head and frowned at Millie.

"Now," Doctor Wade said, taking a blanket off the bed and putting it over Janie's legs. "we're going for a little ride."

Janie folded her hands in her lap and looked down.

After a short trip down the hall the doctor turned and pushed the chair through an open door into a large sun room filled with beautiful green plants and colorful flowers. He rolled the chair up to the large glass window at the far end of the room and stopped.

"Look," he said, pointing toward the outside. "Haven't you missed seeing that?"

"Oh!" Janie caught her breath when she gazed out the window.

The view was breathtaking. Ridges and valleys formed a panoramic view of the mountains all around the hospital. The sun glistening off the trees made it look like a child's kaleidoscope with the colors changing as clouds drifted over the terrain.

Janie's artist's eyes saw every shade of green, yellow and red and made her hands begin to itch to feel the brushes and smell the paints to put this beautiful sight on canvas.

"I am going to survive," she thought. "I will paint again...someday."

And she hoped that she had the strength.

"Pretty, isn't it?" he asked.

Janie nodded slowly and her thoughts went back to the last time she had enjoyed the mountain views...a time when Russ was by her side. Flooded with past memories she suddenly became sad.

"Take me back to my room, please," Janie said softly, her voice breaking.

"Let's stay a little while and enjoy the view. The sun will be setting soon and it will be beautiful."

"No! I want to go now," Janie whispered.

"You must be tired of staying in that same room every day," he said, pulling a chair up close to Janie and sitting down in it. "Let's watch the sunset."

"Take me back to my room!" she demanded quietly. "Now!"

The doctor did not respond.

"Are you going to take me back to my room?" Janie asked, looking at him with tears in her eyes.

"Yes," he answered softly, seeing the tears and then understanding her sudden mood change.

"Thank you," she whispered, hoping the tears filling her eyes would not spill over onto her face.

The doctor leaned close to Janie. "But will you do something for me before we go?" he asked.

Janie shrugged her shoulders.

"My name is Doctor James Wade but my friends call me Jim. It would make me very happy if you call me Jim," he smiled.

Janie shrugged her shoulders again, but didn't look at him.

"The mountains are beautiful, aren't they?" he asked as he stood and turned Janie's chair away from the window.

"Yes," Janie whispered, looked around at the doctor and tried to smile. "Thank you for bringing me here."

"What a beautiful smile," he said as he rolled her back to her room.

After Janie was back in her bed and the doctor had left she reflected on what had happened.

"It was very thoughtful of him to take me to the sun room." she thought. "It wasn't his fault that it caused bad memories. I will apologize when I see him again"

She sighed deeply and closed her eyes letting the memories wash over her. But this time, there were good memories healing her wounded heart with warmth that enfolded her and renewed her strength.

CHAPTER TWENTY-THREE

Following the first trip to the sunroom Janie felt more comfortable venturing out of her room alone and she had been returning to the room daily to enjoy the view of the mountains.

Late one afternoon just before dusk while she watched the sun drop into a beautiful sunset, she heard a voice behind her.

"I thought I might find you here when I saw your room was empty."

She turned quickly and saw Dr. Wade standing behind her.

"May I sit down?" he asked, smiling. "I've been out of town and I've missed this view."

Janie nodded and he pulled a chair close to her side.

"Magnificent, isn't it?" he said, motioning to the mountains while he eased himself down in the chair.

"Yes," Janie answered softly. "I come here every-day to watch the sunset."

"Good."

They sat silently for a moment until Janie turned toward the doctor. "There's something I want to say to you," she began.

"And what is that?" he asked, looking into her eyes.

"It's about my rudeness the day you brought me here."

Janie explained what she had felt that caused her sadness and abrupt request to return to her room.

Even though the doctor knew about the accident and the loss of her husband and baby, he let her talk, knowing this was good therapy for her. He knew her being able to open up to him was a good sign of the inner healing that everyone had been praying to happen. His decision to bring her out of the cocoon of her room had been the right one and he was happy to see this change.

"I do apologize for my behavior," she said, looking at the doctor.

"Apology accepted," he smiled, reaching over and patting her hand. "I understand."

They sat quietly for a while, comfortable in the silence.

Dr. Wade glanced over at Janie and noticed her looking at a long scar on his arm. He looked down at it quickly and rubbed his fingers over it.

"I see that you noticed the little souvenir I got from an Indian Ball Game," he said, laughing softly.

"Indian Ball Game?" Janie asked.

"You're a Cherokee. Don't tell me that you don't know about the game."

"Well, I was reared in Kentucky and...."

"The game is also called Indian Stick Ball," he interrupted.

"Oh...stick ball," Janie laughed, "I've heard about that game."

Dr. Wade was delighted to hear Janie laugh and he smiled broadly.

"I've heard about it, but I've never seen it played."

"It's the oldest ball game in the world."

"Really?" Janie responded, her interest growing.

"Yes...a forerunner of the lacrosse game."

"So, you play the game?"

"Not now...but when I was young I played it often."

"And that's how you got that scar?" she said, pointing to the long jagged scar on his arm.

The doctor nodded.

"Tell me about the game....and the scar," Janie said, intrigued by this new information.

"Well, in one game I got control of the ball and was running with it, far ahead of my opponents...or so I thought....but a man from the other team appeared behind me, knocked me down and pulled me across the field."

"My word," Janie frowned.

"And I ended up with a broken arm and this scar."

"So it must be a lot like football."

Dr. Wade nodded. "Only a lot rougher."

"Please tell me more," Janie said, becoming more interested.

"It's played on a big field. There are no marked sidelines like in football. At each end of the field are two long tree branches placed in the ground. They stand about eight feet apart. To score in the game the player must carry the ball between the branches. The game is won by the first team to score twelve points."

"What kind of ball is used in the game?" Janie said.

"Well, the ball is about the size of a golf ball, but not as hard. Each player has two sticks that have a woven cup on one end of each stick. During the play the ball must be picked up by the two sticks. Then it can be transferred to the hand. A player can throw the ball to a teammate which is usually done when the player is tackled."

"Tackled?"

"Oh, yes! Knocked down, tackled, and pushed...whatever it takes to get the ball."

"Oh, my," Janie said, surprised.

"If a man gets hurt and has to leave the game, a man from the opposing team must leave also. Each team must have an even number of players at all times."

"What kind of uniform do the players wear?"

Dr. Wade smiled. "Just shorts. No shirt, no pads and the players are barefooted."

"Barefooted?" Janie exclaimed.

"Yes, no sissy stuff in stick ball." he smiled.

By now Janie's eyes were wide with amazement. "That game sounds more like a battle than a fun sport. It sounds really dangerous."

"Long ago the game was played to settle disputes between Indian settlements and it was not uncommon for men to be killed during the game."

"You're kidding!" Janie looked at the doctor in disbelief.

"No, it's true, but that doesn't happen anymore."

"But what if a player does something really rough to his opponent in the game?"

"There are two men, called drivers, much like the referees in a football game. Each of them is on the field during the game and carries a long switch. If one of the players does something that is not acceptable the driver warns the player by tapping him with the switch."

"Oh, my!" Janie laughed.

"Now, are you ready for this?" the doctor smiled.

"What?"

"Cherokee women also play the game."

"You're kidding!"

"No." the doctor responded. "Some of them are very good players."

"I would love to see a game. It sounds fascinating."

"The game is played at the Fall Festival in Cherokee. Would you really like to see a game?"

"Yes...when all of these are gone," Janie motioned to the bandages on her face.

"Then I would like to take you," he replied, smiling, ignoring the bandages.

Later, when Janie returned to her room she lay in her bed and thought about her visit with the doctor in the sunroom. She would really like to see a Cherokee Stick Ball Game ...and with him.

CHAPTER TWENTY-FOUR

*E*ach day Janie was healing and becoming stronger. She was attending physical therapy sessions to help her learn to walk again and was making remarkable progress.

Dr. Wade had performed additional minor surgeries to erase the only scars left on her face. The last surgery had been completed and today all of the bandages would come off her face for the final time.

Janie had not seen her face when the bandages were changed and now she was plagued with nervousness about seeing her face again.

"All right!" Millie sang, bursting into the room. "Today's the big day!"

Janie did not respond.

"Look what I brought!" Millie said excitedly.

Millie took her hand from behind her back and held a mirror toward Janie.

"This is for you!" she smiled broadly and offered the mirror to Janie, who did not respond.

"Here! Take this!" Millie said, hopping up on the bed, and leaning back on the pillow. "Dr. Wade will be here soon to take the last bandages off your face."

Slowly Janie reached out and took the mirror from Millie. She laid it face down on the bed beside her.

"Millie, I don't want to see my face," Janie said.

"No?" Millie turned to look at Janie.

Janie shook her head. "No, I don't," Janie said firmly.

"Don't be silly," Millie laughed. "Just wait until the bandages are off," she said while smoothing Janie's hair. "You'll see how beautifully your face has healed."

"I'm scared, Millie."

"Scared? Hey, it's going to be all right," Millie encouraged her friend.

"I don't know. I..."

"Oh, hush!" Millie said, slipping off the bed. "You will look like yourself again."

"Well, I'm nervous," Janie insisted.

"Okay. You can be nervous..." Millie giggled, looking at her friend. "...but not scared."

Janie sighed deeply.

"You know," Millie said thoughtfully, "I've never seen your face."

"I know," Janie said slowly, touching the bandages on her face.

"Well...you just wait and see," Millie said, patting Janie's hand. "You're going to be beautiful."

A soft knock on the door was heard as Dr. Wade walked in.

"How are you feeling today, Janie?" he asked.

"Nervous," she answered quietly.

The doctor patted Janie on the shoulder.

"Well, I want you to relax," he said, smiling "Close your eyes. This won't take long."

Millie took Janie's hand, nodded and smiled at her friend.

Slowly the doctor snipped the bandages from Janie's face. When he finished he stepped back from the bed and smiled.

"Oh, Janie!" Millie gushed, squeezing Janie's hand. "You are so beautiful!"

"Yes, you are," the doctor said in a soft voice, looking at Janie with a smile.

He leaned close to Janie and traced his fingers over her face, then stepped back again and smiled.

Millie picked up the mirror and held it before Janie.

"Look at yourself," she laughed. "Open your eyes."

Slowly Janie's eyes opened and she peered into the mirror at her reflection.

Silence filled the room for a moment.

"Well, what do you think?" Millie asked.

"I don't know what to say," Janie stammered, staring into the mirror.

"Honey, if I looked like you I'd sure know what to say...and do!" Millie whispered.

The doctor caught Millie's comment and grinned.

Janie slowly traced over her face with her fingertips, noting every detail.

"I can't tell anything ever happened to my face. There are no scars and my face is so smooth," she whispered.

"The redness will go away soon," assured the doctor.

"Didn't I tell you a long time ago that Dr. Wade works miracles?" Millie said turning to the doctor and nodding.

Janie's gaze lifted and she looked into her surgeon's eyes.

"Thank you," she smiled "Thank you so much."

"My pleasure," he responded with a smile. "Glad to do it."

Millie grinned at Janie.

"Now, you'll be going home in a couple of days. Your face is fine, but Dr. Tremont said that you might have to walk with a cane for a week, but soon you'll be as good as new," Doctor Wade said.

"Home?" Janie thought. "I don't want to go back to Kentucky."

Janie and Millie watched the doctor leave the room.

Almost as soon as the door closed, it opened again.

Doctor Wade's head appeared from around the half open door.

"I'll see you before you leave the hospital," he said, and then he was gone.

"I'll miss him when I leave here," Janie thought.

"Hey, I've been thinking about something," Millie said.

"What?" Janie asked, looking back at herself in the mirror.

"I've got an idea. Why don't you come to my

house and stay with me for a while when you leave here?"

"With you?" Janie asked, lowering the mirror to look at Millie.

"Sure. I have plenty of room."

"Well, maybe...I..."

Millie interrupted. "Say yes! I would love to have you."

"I don't know...I'll think about it," Janie said, looking into the mirror again.

Janie was so engrossed with her restored features that she didn't realize Millie had left to finish her duties. Looking at her face she was amazed that she bore no physical signs of the terrible accident that had robbed her of so much. She knew that this was her face, yet she saw small changes in her features. As Janie gazed into the mirror she wondered if she was finding small changes in her emotions as well. Could her handsome doctor also be responsible for these feelings? She immediately dismissed these thoughts as betrayal...or were they the strength of survival?

Time...only time....

CHAPTER TWENTY-FIVE

*M*illie and Janie sat in the swing on Millie's front porch enjoying the view in front of them.

The crisp fall day and the leaves of reds, golds and yellows made a bright display of colors in front of them. The poplar and the red maple trees around Millie's house were glowing brilliantly in the October sunshine. Their beauty had beckoned Millie and Janie to enjoy their morning coffee outside.

Janie had been staying with Millie for almost a month and now the time was nearing when she knew that she must leave the mountains and go back to Kentucky.

She wanted to begin painting again soon. She missed her work.

"The mountains are so beautiful," Janie sighed. "The colors are breathtaking. They make me want to paint again."

Millie turned quickly to look at Janie.

"I didn't know you are an artist. Why hasn't someone mentioned this?"

"It's a long story, Millie," Janie smiled, "for another day."

Millie nodded, and they enjoyed the view in silence for a while.

"My mother loved the leaf season," Janie said. "I wish she was here to see the leaves now."

"Janie, you've never said much about your mother. I know you must miss her," Millie said.

"Yes," Janie responded quietly. "You know about my father, but I never told you how my father and mother met, did I?"

"No."

"It was at an Indian Pow Wow in Oklahoma."

Millie nodded and took another sip of coffee.

"Mother was smitten by the handsome young Cherokee man the first time she saw him. She fell instantly in love with him. He completely swept her off her feet and they were married in Oklahoma two weeks after they met."

"Two weeks?" Millie turned to look at Janie.

Janie nodded.

"When Mother returned home with a husband Grandmother Rose and Granddaddy Lone Wolf were shocked. My parents stayed with my grandparents for a while, but my father couldn't find work. He had a friend in Kentucky who offered him a job so they went there to live. I was born soon after the move. Mother said that Daddy worked hard for the first few years of their marriage." Janie paused and took a sip of coffee before she continued.

"Emily and Hunter were born in Kentucky and, well, you know the rest of the story."

Millie nodded.

Janie rose and walked to the porch railing and looked out at the mountains for a moment then returned to a chair and began rocking.

"He just couldn't take the responsibility of a family anymore," Janie added, shaking her head from side to side.

The two friends sat in silence for a short time enjoying the beauty of the distant mountains.

"I'm going down to see Grandmother Rose for a while, Millie," Janie said, interrupting their reverie. "I appreciate all you've done for me. You are really a good friend."

"What about Doctor Wade?"

"What about him?"

During Janie's visit with Millie Doctor Wade had called Janie several times, inquiring about her convalescence... inviting her out for a ride...or dinner with him. Each time Janie had thanked him and politely refused.

"I've been dismissed from all my doctors and need to think about going back to Kentucky soon," Janie replied, obviously evading Millie's question.

"I understand, but I sure will miss you."

Millie was never one to keep still when she had a mission so she jumped right in where she had been treading softly and demanded an explanation.

"Oh, Janie, why don't you give yourself a chance to know him? He's a fine person."

Janie was startled by her friend's outburst. She couldn't explain to Millie her mixed feelings of guilt and wonder so she didn't look at Millie for fear of revealing her confusion. Instead she shrugged her shoulders indifferently.

CHAPTER TWENTY-SIX

*S*ince returning to Kentucky Janie had visited with friends and tried to enjoy being in her gallery again, but without Russ in the shop it didn't hold the pleasure that it once did for her...and she was lonely.

Emily and Hunter had successfully operated the gallery while she was away, but now with her return they left the shop to follow their own interests.

Emily had married soon after Janie's return and moved to Iowa with her husband. Hunter had gone to New Mexico to study at the Indian Institute of Art. Now the gallery was Janie's full responsibility.

Janie stayed busy at her store, but she missed her friend, Millie and Grandmother Rose...and she missed the mountains. She and Millie talked to each other on the telephone almost every day, but it wasn't the same as being with her friend. On each call Millie would tell Janie how much she missed her and begged her friend to return to the mountains.

Today Janie had finally made an important decision...one she had been struggling over for weeks... and now she was anxious to share it with Millie. She smiled as she dialed Millie's number, knowing that her friend would be pleased with the news.

"Millie!" she said excitedly, as soon as Millie answered the phone. "I'm coming back to North Carolina!"

"What?"

"I'm coming back to North Carolina!" Janie said excitedly.

"Great! How long can you stay?" Millie asked.

"Forever!" Janie laughed.

"What?"

"Forever! I'm going to sell my house and move to the mountains."

"That's great news!" Millie laughed. "What about the gallery?"

"I think I know someone who will buy it. He's been after me to sell the shop to him for years."

"When are you coming?"

"Soon. I want to look for a house to buy."

"Good," Millie laughed. "I'll start looking for one near me!"

"Millie," Janie said softly, "I'm planning to live near Grandmother Rose."

"Oh?"

"Yes. She's getting older now and I want to be near her."

"Okay, I understand," Millie said. "You'll only be an hour away from me."

"That's right," Janie agreed.

"I can handle that!" Millie laughed. She could hardly wait for Janie to get back.

The next few weeks were busy ones for Janie. She was delighted when her house and gallery sold almost as soon as they were placed on the market. She made two trips to the mountains before she found a house she liked, and she purchased it immediately.

Rose was delighted and looked forward to having her granddaughter living in one of the new cabins that had been built near her. The move took place quickly and Millie had come for a few days to help Janie get settled in her new home.

The cabin, surrounded by a panoramic view of the mountains, sat on a rise overlooking the river. A wide porch ran all the way around the house and a large fire pot on the back deck made it possible to enjoy the mountain views all year. The rooms were large and airy with high ceilings with wide beams. A large stone fireplace in the living room kept the space cozy and inviting. Large windows in every room gave breath-taking views in all seasons and the Native

American furnishings and quilts mixed with Janie's personal treasures and artwork made the cabin both comfortable and unique. One of the first things Janie had placed in her new home was the hiking stick. The cabin had already taken on a personality of its own and would be a healing place for Janie...and she was glad to be living close to her grandmother. Janie knew Grandmother was a wise woman and she wanted to learn more from her.

Millie and Janie were taking a break from their work in the cabin to sit on the front porch and rest for a while. They sat with their feet propped up on the railing gazing at the mountains and sipping a cup of hot tea.

"Janie, I've been meaning to ask you about the stick you use when you go hiking...the one that was in your hospital room. It's so beautiful hanging over your mantle."

Janie stared out over the railing for a few minutes wondering where to begin and finally decided the best place to start any story was at the very beginning.

"If you get bored just hold up your hands and I'll stop. This story goes back a long, long way."

Millie was intrigued and knew she wouldn't get bored.

Janie first told her about White Feather and her family and their journey on the Trail of Tears and how White Feather had finally made her way back home to the mountains. She continued her story with the legend of the Cherokee Rose.

She stopped, looked at Millie and asked "Are you sure you want to hear all of this?"

Millie was intrigued. "Please...go on."

Janie sipped her tea and began again. She told Millie how her grandmother had come to Cherokee to teach school, met Lone Wolf and his grandfather, Walking Eagle.

"It was Walking Eagle who gave the stick to Grandmother Rose and told her its history. He told her that the stick had been carved by Tsu-la (Red Fox) as a gift for White Feather after her husband, Running

Deer, had died on the march to Oklahoma. Tsu–la was their good friend and knew how much White Feather missed her husband and their home."

Janie stopped again and glanced over at Millie who sat enthralled with the story.

"Don't stop now, Janie," she prompted. "I have to know how the stick has been passed down for such a long time."

Janie laughed at Millie and said, "Okay, here's how it happened. After White Feather's death the stick belonged to her daughter, Little Fawn, who, much later gave it to Tsu-la's granddaughter who in turn gave it to Walking Eagle when he was a very young boy because he was a descendant of Tsu-la."

Janie paused for a moment, blew out a long breath, then added, "And of course, you know the rest of the story...how Grandmother Rose gave me the stick on my wedding day and how important its meaning has become to me"

Janie paused and laughed. "Whew! I told you it was a long story."

"I loved it!" Millie replied.

Janie grew wishful now thinking about the loss of Russ and the unborn baby and said almost in a whisper, "Maybe Emily or Hunter will have a little girl one day and I can pass the stick on to her."

"Or maybe you will," Millie remarked with a smile.

The two friends sat quietly for a while finishing their tea.

"Janie?" Millie said, interrupting their thoughts.
"Yes?"

"Janie, do you ever think about Doctor Wade?"
"Who?"

"Your surgeon," Millie said, turning to look at Janie.

"Oh, occasionally, I guess," Janie answered shrugging her shoulders indifferently.

"You know, Janie, he was really smitten by you," Millie said seriously.

Janie laughed. "Well, I don't know about that."

"Well, I do," Millie said. "Why wouldn't you go out

with him?"

"Oh, Millie, I don't know. He's very nice, but..."

"But what? He's called you to go for a ride or go out to dinner with him and you've turned him down every time."

"And," interrupted Janie, "he's probably given up," she laughed. "Now let's talk about something else."

"All right, but I still think that you should give him a chance," Millie insisted.

Janie leaned back in her chair and folded her arms. "I've been thinking about having a housewarming...maybe a little dinner party to celebrate my new home," she said, changing the subject. "What do you think?"

"I think that's a great idea," responded Millie enthusiastically.

"I want you to come. And I thought that I'd invite Grandmother Rose and Tara and Steve."

"Sounds like a nice group. Do you mind if I bring someone with me?" Millie asked eagerly.

"No. I don't mind."

"Thanks."

"Who are you bringing?" Janie asked.

"You'll see," Millie answered with a playful smile on her face.

"Tell me."

"No!"

"Why are you being so secretive?" Janie smiled.

"You'll see!" Millie laughed.

"I bet it's a new boyfriend," Janie teased her friend.

"You'll see." Millie repeated, smiling at her friend.

"You're not going to tell me?" Janie asked.

"Nope! Now, come on, we've got to get back to work or this cabin will never be ready for the party," Millie said, jumping out of her chair and grabbing Janie by the hand.

A soft breeze rose up from the river below and they both stopped to watch a small white feather drift along in the air in front of the deck. A shiver ran along Janie's spine at the sight and a warm feeling

washed over her body.
She smiled.

CHAPTER TWENTY-SEVEN

*J*anie's guests were due to arrive any minute and she was excited about her housewarming party. She was anxious to show off her new home to Tara and Steve. Grandmother Rose had already arrived and was in the kitchen bustling about.

And Janie could hardly wait to meet the mysterious guest Millie was bringing. She hoped her friend had found a good person to share her life and she looked forward to meeting him. She saw two cars driving up the winding narrow road so she hurried out on the front porch to greet them.

Tara and Steve came up the walk first and as Janie was hugging and welcoming them to her home her voice halted for a moment. Following Millie up the walk was her mystery guest. No wonder her friend had kept him a secret! It was Jim Wade-her Doctor Wade!

With all the confusion of greetings and hugs there was no time to find out about this turn of events. She could hardly wait to get Millie alone and hear the news. She knew her friend had been taken by the handsome doctor, and ...she certainly intended to find out more after dinner.

"That was a delicious meal, Janie," Steve said. "Thank you."

"Yes," echoed all the people seated around the table.

"Would you like to have coffee and dessert out on the deck?" Janie asked her guests.

"Yes, let's do that," Rose responded. "It's such a beautiful warm evening."

The others all agreed and they rose from the table

and followed Rose outside.

As everyone left the room Janie took Millie's arm.

"Want to give me a hand, Millie?" Janie asked.

"Sure."

When they arrived in the kitchen Janie quietly closed the door and pulled Millie to her side.

"Millie, when did the two of you start dating?" she whispered.

"What?"

"You and Dr. Wade. When did you start dating him?"

Millie broke into quiet laughter and put her hand over her mouth. She shook her head from side to side.

"Shh. Why are you laughing?" Janie asked, leaning close to her friend. "What's the matter?"

"I'm laughing at you," Millie snickered.

"Me?"

"Yes! You! I don't date Dr. Wade. I brought him here tonight for you!"

"For me?"

"Yes, you – silly. He's your housewarming gift from me!" she laughed softly.

"Oh, Millie," Janie turned and began putting slices of cake on small plates. "I don't know what to think of you!"

"Well, it seemed the only way I could get you two together," Millie said, placing the cake plates on a tray.

"Millie..."

Millie interrupted. "The man has been trying so hard to see you, Janie. He's told me that he has called you on the phone over and over many times since you left the hospital...even while you were living in Kentucky."

"Yes...called to see how I'm healing from the surgery."

"Yes, but..." Millie answered, pouring coffee into the cups on the tray. "I didn't think you would mind if I brought him tonight."

"No, I don't mind, Millie, but..."

Millie took the coffee pot from Janie and set it on

the counter. She put her hands on Janie's shoulders and turned her friend so that they were facing each other. Millie looked straight into Janie's eyes.

"Janie," Millie said seriously. "It's been almost three years since Russ died. You're young. It's time to move on."

Janie looked down and shook her head slowly from side to side.

"You like Dr. Wade, don't you, Janie?" Millie asked.

"Yes. He's very nice."

"Well, give him a chance," urged Millie.

"I don't know," Janie said slowly.

"Don't you ever get lonesome up here on the mountain...living by yourself?"

"Well." Janie looked away from Millie, "...sometimes."

"Then let him be your friend. He's a good man, Janie, and I know he cares for you," Millie said, placing her hand on Janie's arm. "Go out with him the next time he invites you."

"I don't know, Millie." Janie looked down.

"Think about it," pleaded Millie.

"All right, but what about you? Don't you want someone special in your life?"

A wide grin spread across Millie's face.

"I have someone, Janie," she replied, smiling.

"What?" Janie turned quickly to face her friend.

Millie nodded, her smile widening.

"Why haven't you told me?" Janie scolded good-naturally.

"I wanted to be sure how we felt about each other first."

"Why didn't you bring him tonight?"

"Because I wanted to bring the doctor for you," Millie laughed.

"Millie," Janie said, shaking her head and returning Millie's laugh. "You are something else!"

The two friends hugged.

"Why don't you stay tonight and tell me all about this new boyfriend? I'll take you home tomorrow,"

Janie said.

"Sounds like a good plan to me," laughed Millie.

Janie picked up the tray and left the kitchen with a smiling Millie trailing behind.

CHAPTER TWENTY-EIGHT

*T*wo days after the housewarming party Janie was napping in the warm sunshine on her front porch when the telephone rang shrilly, awaking her.

"Hello," she said breathlessly, after rushing into the house to answer the call.

"Hello. And how are you today?"

"Fine," she answered, recognizing the voice immediately.

"Sounds like you must have run to the phone," he laughed.

"Well, no, I didn't run...just hurried a little. I was out on the porch."

"Did I catch you at a bad time?"

"No."

"I'll get right to the point."

"Oh?"

"Yes. I've called you to ask you to have dinner with me Friday night in Ashville."

"I don't know..." Janie hesitated.

"I'm not going to take no for an answer," he interrupted.

Janie politely refused his invitation, but he was very persuasive and she finally agreed to meet him for dinner. She was positive he had that familiar smile on his face now.

After the call ended Janie immediately dialed Millie's number.

"I know Miss Cupid will be pleased I finally gave in to the doctor's invitation," Janie thought and chuckled while waiting for Millie to answer. "I'm sure she won't mind my waking her."

"Hello," Millie murmured sleepily after rolling over in bed and fumbling for the receiver.

"Sorry to wake you, Millie. I know you are working long night hours at the hospital this week, but I need to ask you something."

"Okay."

"How would you like to have me for an overnight guest on Friday night?"

"Fine with me," Millie answered with a yawn.

"I have a dinner date in Ashville."

"Okay. I'll see you then," Millie said, yawning again, anxious to go back to sleep.

"Thanks."

Millie moved to hang up the phone, then quickly sat up in bed and brought the receiver back to her mouth.

"Wait a minute, Janie," she said loudly. "Janie! Janie!"

"Yes?" Janie said smiling, still holding the phone to her ear, waiting for Millie's delayed response.

"Did you say you have a date?"

"Yes."

"With Dr. Wade, I hope."

"Yes, Ms. Cupid!" Janie laughed.

"Great! It's about time."

"Go back to sleep. I'll see you Friday."

Janie quietly hung up the phone and glanced at the small wooden turtle sitting on the table in front of her. Dr. Wade had given it to her for a housewarming gift and she remembered how surprised she had been to learn he had carved it. She picked up the carving and looked at the delicate designs engraved on it. She turned it over and over in her hands, admiring its beauty. She smiled at the turtle, and then placed it back on the table.

Leaning back on the sofa she crossed her arms in front of herself and frowned.

"Well, one little dinner shouldn't be too hard," she thought, and then added, "and he does seem to be a very nice man."

"Silly schoolgirl," Janie chided herself as she

began to giggle. The giggle soon turned to outright laughter...laughter of sheer joy and anticipation. She jumped up from the sofa and did a little dance around the room.

"Now, what shall I wear?"

CHAPTER TWENTY-NINE

*J*anie had wondered if being alone with the doctor for the first time away from the hospital would be awkward, but the feeling had quickly vanished. She was very comfortable with him and the evening had gone well.

"Jim, this is a lovely inn and restaurant," Janie said, smiling.

"I thought you'd like it here. It's one of my favorite places in Ashville," he replied, pleased to hear Janie call him by his first name.

"And the scenery is beautiful," Janie remarked, motioning toward the window where the mountains could be seen in the distance.

They had finished their meals just as the sunset was approaching.

"Wait until you see the sunset here. It's spectacular," said Jim.

"I'm looking forward to it," Janie smiled.

"That's a beautiful turquoise nugget you're wearing," Jim observed.

"Thank you. It belonged to my father," Janie responded caressing the nugget with her fingers

"Tell me about yourself, Janie," Jim said softly, looking into her eyes.

"Oh, there's not much to tell," she replied with a slight smile. "You know my medical history."

"I'm not talking about your medical history," he smiled back. "I want to know about YOU."

"All right, but I warn you, it's pretty dull," she said, placing her coffee cup back in the saucer and folding her hands in her lap, she began. "I attended college after high school and after graduating I worked as a buyer for a large Native American Art Gallery for a while. Then I married my college sweetheart. We saved our money and purchased our own gallery. Mother died soon after our marriage and then we took care of my younger brother and sister and...well, you know the rest."

Jim leaned slightly toward Janie."There's one thing you didn't mention."

"And what is that?"

"You didn't say you are a Native American...a Cherokee Indian."

"Well, I am," she said, her dark eyes looking into Jim's face. "I am very proud of my heritage."

"Did you know that I'm a Cherokee also?" he asked.

"No," Janie said slowly, looking closely at him and thinking that she should have already realized his heritage...the dark skin, black hair and eyes, and the stick ball game.

"I was born fifty miles from here. I grew up on the Qualla Boundary ...the Cherokee Indian Reservation. I have family living there."

"Really?"

"Yes."

"Tell me more," she laughed softly.

"I went to college, medical school, interned, went back to medical school, specialized in plastic surgery," he held his arms open at his sides, "and here I am."

"As one of the most well-known surgeons in your medical field," Janie said, "and very much in demand, I hear...and very much appreciated by this lady,"

Jim looked down and Janie thought she saw him blush under his dark-complexioned skin.

For a moment there was silence between them.

"May I ask you a personal question?" Janie asked.

"Certainly," he responded, smiling.

"Have you ever been married?"

Jim picked up his coffee cup, took a sip, and put it back down on the table.

He did not respond immediately.

"Oh, I'm sorry," Janie said apologetically, thinking

that she had offended him and wishing that she had not asked such a personal question.

"No, that's all right." He hesitated, and then continued, "I came close to getting married one time, but it didn't work out, thank goodness."

He looked directly at Janie eyes.

"My finance liked being a social butterfly...traveling, going to parties..." he looked down and fumbled with the linen napkin on the table "...and she didn't understand the demands of my chosen profession. I traveled quite a bit as I do now, and she wanted me home all the time to escort her to parties and vacation trips." He paused for a moment. "I wanted children...she did not."

Janie shook her head slowly from side to side and looked down.

"Well, anyway it just didn't work out," Jim concluded. "Looking back I realize that we would never have had a good married life together."

"I'm sorry," Janie said softly, looking up into Jim's eyes.

"Oh, don't be. It was good we broke up before we married. Actually, I don't think we were really in love."

Janie sat silently, watching the doctor's eyes as he spoke.

"My years of medical training and study have left little time for dating. I've had a few dates, but none of the women kept my interest long enough for a committed relationship," he said, thinking that no woman had attracted his attention and held it until Janie came along.

"Would you like to have dessert?" the waiter asked, pausing at the table.

"Janie?" Jim asked.

"None for me, thank you," replied Janie.

"Janie, do you like to fly?" Jim asked suddenly.

"Pardon?"

"Do you like to ride in an airplane?"

Janie shrugged her shoulders slightly. "I suppose...although I've never flown much."

"Would you like to go flying sometime?"

"Umm...I don't know...maybe," she answered.

"I have a plane and..."

"You own an airplane?" Janie interrupted, smiling and wondering if he was teasing her.

"Yes, and I fly it," he laughed softly, somewhat amused at her question.

"And you fly it?" she smiled.

"Yes. When I have surgeries scheduled at hospitals in other cities I have my own transportation," he smiled. "Now, I ask you again. Would you like to go up sometime?"

"Well, maybe," she answered with a teasing glitter in her eyes.

"Fine," he smiled, reaching across the table for her hand. His fingers lingered for a moment and he looked into her eyes with a glimmer of hope in his own.

"Come, let's walk down to the lower level of the terrace and enjoy the beautiful sunset."

As they rose they swayed toward each other and then slowly apart while their eyes locked for a moment. Then, resisting a mad urge to take Janie into his arms, he took her hand and led her away from the table before he embarrassed them both. Neither of them could resist a giggle as they left the room.

Janie enjoyed the remainder of the weekend visiting Millie. It was Sunday and Janie knew she would have to leave for home soon.

"Janie, I haven't asked you, but did you enjoy your date with Doctor Wade?" Millie asked, while the two friends sat on Millie's porch enjoying the afternoon's warm sunshine.

Janie smiled. She had wondered how long her curious friend would wait before she asked about the date.

"Yes, I did," Janie responded with a smile, suppressing the urge to giggle.

"Are you going to see him again?"

"Millie! You are so inquisitive!" Janie scolded her friend good -naturedly.

"Well! Are you?"

Janie shifted in the chair and looked away from

Millie.

"Oh, I don't know," she replied indifferently, not ready to share her feelings yet...not even with Millie.

Millie leaned toward Janie.

"But you would go out with him again if he asked you, wouldn't you?"

"Millie, can we talk about something else, please?" Janie pleaded.

"Sure," Millie nodded, knowing that she would get no more information at this time.

"I think I should start for home," Janie said, looking at her watch.

"Let's get together again real soon," Millie said, as the two friends hugged. "You're welcome anytime."

When Janie arrived home she decided to walk down to the river before dark. Choosing a place beside the river where the water ebbed into tiny whirlpools on its journey down from the high mountains, she sank down on the soft grass. She drew her knees up to her chest, circled her arms around her knees and laid her cheek on the skirt that covered her legs. This was her special place and she spent many hours here thinking about her new life and painting her landscapes.

"Such a peaceful place," she thought as she gazed around her.

Twilight had come early so Janie returned to her cabin after a short while. She sat with her feet propped up on the banister rail of her cabin's front porch. She leaned back and reflected on the weekend she had spent in Ashville as she watched the sun disappear behind the mountains.

The dinner with Jim had been enjoyable. When he suggested that their date be repeated the next night she had felt disappointed that she could not accept his invitation. She and Millie had made plans for Saturday night and she didn't want to disappoint her friend, even for the man who stirred these new feelings. There would be time...maybe.

Gazing at the river Janie saw a faint movement

near the water on the opposite side. She put her feet on the floor, stood and leaned forward on the railing to try to get a better look. She peered into the darkness for a long time but didn't see it again.

She turned and started into her cabin just as the telephone rang.

"Hello," she answered, wondering if it was Jim and found herself hoping that it was him.

"And hello to you too, pretty lady."

When the caller spoke, Janie immediately recognize his voice and smiled.

It was a long time before the conversation ended and Janie found her way to bed.

Her rest was filled with unusual dreams of floating on clouds of white feathers with Jim by her side.

CHAPTER THIRTY

*J*anie stood at the window of her home gazing at the mountains and the cloudless blue sky while she drank her first cup of coffee of the day. She had been happy living in her new home for the past several months and especially enjoyed living near her Grandmother Rose. Millie was a frequent visitor and Jim had come to see her several times since their dinner date.

The woods and mountains around Janie's house beckoned her daily and she looked forward to hiking in the woods around her home each day.

"Today is perfect for hiking," she thought as she got her stick and left the cabin to begin her trek through the woods.

After her daily hikes ended she always enjoyed a quiet rest beside the river. She loved listening to the water rushing over the river rocks while it splashed its way down the mountain stream. The birds' songs and the woodpeckers in the distance hammering on trees always captivated her senses while the squirrels scampering about among the trees brought a smile,

Today she had hiked further than usual and she was glad when she returned to her place of rest. She leaned the stick against a tree, wiped the moisture from her brow and sank down on the cool grass beside the river. She put her hands on the ground behind her and leaned back on her elbows. Tilting her head upward she closed her eyes for a moment and let the sun bathe her face with its warmth. She stood and moved to a tree and sat down, then leaned back against its trunk and yawned. The warm sunshine and the sound of the moving water made Janie sleepy and she closed her eyes. The soft mossy grass and the pungent smells surrounding her soon relaxed her body and she drifted into a light sleep.

Suddenly she heard a movement near her. Her eyes sprung open and she sat up quickly but saw no one.

"Probably a deer going to the water," she thought. She smiled and leaned back. The sound of the rushing water captured her senses and she closed her eyes.

When she heard the sound again her eyes opened quickly. She stood up while her gaze swept across the woods around her. She saw no one but she had the feeling that she was not alone.

"It could be a bear," she thought, remembering that there were bears in the area.

Janie had never been frightened in the woods before, but now she was beginning to feel a bit apprehensive. Oh, how she missed Wa-Yah. He would have kept her safe.

"I'm just being silly," she thought. "I'm not going to let this spoil my outing. I love coming to the river."

She moved to sit down again when another movement nearby caught her attention. She looked quickly to the tree where she thought she had seen movement, but saw nothing. She turned to hurry away. Glancing back over her shoulder she was surprised to see a man suddenly appear from behind the tree.

"Wait! Don't leave!" he called.

Janie stopped and turned around.

An old man stood beside the tree, his hand resting on its trunk.

Janie did not speak.

The man emerged from beside the tree and started walking toward her and Janie could tell from his slow labored steps that he was very old.

As he came nearer Janie looked closely at him and noticed that he wore tattered jeans with a hole in the knee of one of the pants legs and he had on a black tee-shirt. She saw that the sneakers he wore on his feet were well-worn, apparently having seen many steps. He wore a black felt hat with a beaded band around its brim with a large feather tucked in the brim also. He wore the hat tilted to the side over his long gray hair which was pulled back and tied in a pony tail. The only jewelry he wore was a watch with a silver band decorated with coral and turquoise stones.

When he reached Janie he stopped before her and smiled.

"Who are you?" Janie asked quickly.

"I won't hurt you," he said softly, moving closer to Janie.

"I said, who are you?" Janie repeated louder. "Where did you come from?"

"Whoa," he chuckled, clearly amused at Janie's questions. "Too many questions at one time."

"Are you lost?" Janie asked, looking straight into his eyes.

"No. I know where I am," he laughed softly, smiling at Janie with a crooked grin. "And I know who I am too," he teased.

Janie was beginning to become annoyed by his casual behavior, but she was strangely drawn to the old man.

"Okay! So who are you and how did you get here?" she asked impatiently.

"I walked out of the woods and here I am!" he teased again, sitting down on a fallen log.

"I've never seen you here before."

"I live several miles back in the mountains," he said, pointing over his shoulder.

"Well, I live in that cabin up there," Janie said, nodding to her home, "and I've never seen you around here."

"You've got a pretty place up there," he nodded toward Janie's house, changing the subject.

Janie was clearly perplexed by the old man's sudden appearance. She wondered if he was lost and perhaps had family looking for him. As they continued to talk Janie's fear of him began to subside even more, but she was still aggravated by his indifference in identifying himself.

"Can I help you find your home and your people?"

she asked.

"Well, thank you, but I don't have any family living near here and I know how to get home," he smiled.

Again Janie realized that the old man was making fun of her questions and she turned and walked away.

"Stay! Don't go! I won't hurt you. I like to have someone to talk to every now and then."

"No! I'm going home...and I want you to go home also," she said firmly. She turned and started walking up the rise to her cabin.

After a short distance she glanced back toward the river.

The log where the old man had sat was empty. She gazed across the woods on the other side of the water and then up and down the river. The old man was nowhere to be seen.

"That's strange," she thought to herself. "How did he disappear so quickly?"

Walking home she shook her head from side to side, wondering if she had fallen asleep and dreamed about the old man...or was he real?"

CHAPTER THIRTY-ONE

*T*he next day the rain began before dawn and lasted all day.

Janie missed her daily walk. Often she would walk to the big glass window in her living room and glance toward the river to see if she could see any signs of the old man.

"I'm being foolish," she scolded herself. "He wouldn't be out in the rain anyway...if I really saw an old man."

The following day dawned cloudy and gray but Janie was encouraged when the sun popped out around noon. She took her hiking stick and went directly to the place where she had seen the old man and sat down on a fallen log near the water and waited, thinking he might appear again. By evening, she had seen no one.

After a week of returning to the same place each day the old man had not appeared and Janie was disappointed. She chastised herself for thinking that he was real, but still she was unsettled about the incident...dream or no dream.

Suddenly Janie thought of her grandmother.

"Grandmother Rose! I must talk to her about this! She will understand!"

She drove quickly to her grandmother's house and bounded through the front door of Rose's cabin, calling her name.

"Just in time!" Rose said with a laugh, hugging Janie. "I'm baking."

"Ummm..." Janie said. "Smells good."

"I'm making cookies. Come on. Let's go in the kitchen. I'll get you a cup of coffee."

Janie followed Rose and sat down at the kitchen table.

Rose put the last of the cookies into the oven to bake and sat down across the table from her grand-daughter.

"How are you, Janie?"

"Good," Janie responded, smiling.

"Now, tell me all the news. Are you still dating the handsome doctor?"

Janie laughed. "Off and on. He's out of town a lot."

"Well, don't let him get away! I think you two belong together," Rose said, standing and placing a cup of coffee in front of Janie.

"Oh, you do? Do you?" Janie laughed.

Rose nodded, smiling at her granddaughter.

"Grandmother, I have had a very strange dream...or at least, I think it must have been a dream."

"A dream?"

"Yes. While I was resting by the river after my hike I think I fell asleep and dreamed about meeting an old Indian man."

"What did he look like?"

After Janie described the man, Rose asked, "Why do you think it was a dream?"

"Well, he hasn't returned. I've been back to the river practically every day and I haven't seen him again."

Rose smiled.

"I'm very confused about the dream," Janie said, frowning.

"Oh, it wasn't a dream, honey," Rose replied.

"How do you know, Grandmother?"

"That was Old Jess."

"Who?"

"Old Jess. I thought I told you about him."

Janie's eyes widen in surprise. "Then, he's real?"

"As real as real can be," Rose laughed.

"So he wasn't a dream, after all," Janie said slowly.

"Nope!" Rose said. "He's real."

"He frightened me a little at first," Janie confessed, "especially when he appeared so suddenly."

"Don't be afraid of him," Rose said, reaching across the table to Janie's hand. "He's harmless."

"Who is he?"

"Well, he's a Cherokee Indian. He's been around here for a very long time."

"Really?"

Rose nodded and got up to take the cookies out of the oven.

"Where does he live, Grandmother?"

"Way up in the mountains. He has a little cabin up there and lives by himself." Rose said, putting a plate of cookies in front of Janie.

"At his age?" Janie asked, taking a cookie.

Rose nodded. "Yes."

"Doesn't he have family?"

"Oh, yes."

"And they don't mind him living alone way out in the woods?" Janie asked, helping herself to another cookie.

"No, they understand his love for being in the woods and living in the little cabin. They come out here and check on him often."

"What does he do when the ice and snow come?" Janie asked. "It gets so cold out in the mountains."

"Oh, he has a house in town and he lives in it during the cold season," explained Rose.

"He's very old, isn't he?"

"Yes. Why, when he was just a boy, right out of high school, he enlisted in the Navy and served in World War Two."

"My word! He is old."

"Yes."

"I wonder if I will ever see him again," Janie said, thoughtfully.

"Most probably...and don't be afraid of him. He's a good man...a respected Cherokee elder. And he has many stories to share," added Rose. "He's a good storyteller."

Two weeks passed before Janie saw Old Jess

again. He appeared quietly, unspeaking, and this time Janie welcomed him.

She was sitting by the river when he appeared. "Grandmother told me about you, and..." Janie began.

"She has told me about you also, Janie," he interrupted with a smile, "a long time ago."

"I haven't seen you in quite a while," Janie began as she watched Old Jess ease himself down on the grass and then she sat down close to him.

They both leaned back against the log like old companions enjoying each other's company.

Janie waited for Old Jess to speak, but the silence was not at all uncomfortable. It was if they had known each other forever.

After Old Jess rested for a bit he began to speak.

"The trip from my cabin is too far for me to walk everyday."

Janie nodded.

"Sometimes these old legs have to rest," he laughed softly.

"Could I ask you something?" Janie asked.

"Yes" he responded.

"Do you mind if I ask you your age?"

"My age?"

Janie nodded. "How old are you?"

"I can't count that high," he said with a chuckle, his eyes crinkling, showing he was amused by his own answer.

Janie laughed.

"I am eighty-five years old," Old Jess said.

"Don't you mind living alone?" Janie continued, wanting to learn more about this unusual man and thinking she would love to paint him.

"I'm never alone," he assured her.

"But..." Janie began.

Old Jess stopped her with upraised hands. "Patience, Janie, all in good time." And with this Old Jess stood and walked into the woods, waving to Janie over his shoulder as he disappeared.

She stayed a while longer thinking about Old Jess and wondering when she would see him again. She felt magnetism toward him she didn't yet understand. Like he said, "All in good time...."

CHAPTER THIRTY-TWO

*J*anie went to the river everyday and waited for Old Jess to appear. She had not seen him for several days and was anxious to talk with him again. Finally, after waiting for almost an hour, he appeared. She eagerly rose to her feet and waved to him before he crossed the river.

Waving back to her, Old Jess carefully stepped on rocks in the river and easily crossed the water while Janie watched in amazement at his agility.

When he reached Janie she motioned for him to sit down beside her on the blanket she had spread on the ground for them.

"How are you today?" she asked.

"Good," he replied, easing himself down on the blanket.

"I've missed you," Janie said, smiling.

"I've been going fishing a lot lately."

Janie nodded. "Have any luck?" she asked.

"Yes," he answered with a grin.

"I brought sandwiches and lemonade for us," Janie said, picking up the picnic basket sitting near-by. "Are you hungry?"

He nodded while he watched Janie take the food out of the basket.

"Looks good," he said, grinning, picking up a sandwich.

They ate in silence for a moment, and then Janie spoke.

"Old Jess, last night I heard a noise on my front porch and I went to the door and opened it to look out. Do you know what I saw?"

The old man shook his head from side to side as

he picked up his drink.

"A big, fat possum," she laughed.

"Do you know the Cherokee story about the possum's tail?" Old Jess asked.

"No, I don't," Janie answered.

"Would you like to hear it?"

"Oh, yes. Please tell it to me," Janie requested, remembering that her grandmother had said Old Jess was a good storyteller.

Old Jess cleared his throat and began...

"Well, the Possum used to have a long, bushy tail and he was very proud of it. He would comb and brush it every day and then go out and tell all the animals how beautiful it was.

"Now Rabbit got tired of hearing Possum brag and boast about his beautiful tail so he decided he would play a trick on the possum.

"There was to be a big party and dance the next day for all the animals in the forest and Rabbit was appointed to go out and spread the news. So the first place he went was to see Possum and tell him about the dance.

"After Rabbit told Possum about the dance Possum said that if he came to the party he would have to have a special seat where he could show off his beautiful tail.

"Rabbit agreed to the seat and told Possum that he could dance too. And then added that he would send someone to comb and brush Possum's tail and help him get ready for the dance.

"Then the rabbit went to see the little cricket. Cricket was an expert hair dresser and Rabbit told the Cricket what he wanted him to do. Cricket smiled and agreed to follow Rabbit's request."

Old Jess stopped, smiled and took a sip of his lemonade, then continued with the story.

"Cricket went to Possum's house early the next morning and told him that he had come to help him get ready to go to the party. He told Possum to stretch out, relax and close his eyes and he would go to work.

"Cricket combed out Possum's tail and wrapped a red string around it. Now all the time he was wrapping Possum's tail he was clipping off the hair close to the roots and Possum never knew it."

"Oh, NO!" Janie laughed.

Old Jess nodded, chuckling.

"Cricket told Possum to leave the red string around his tail to keep it smooth until he was ready to dance.

"Now, when it was time for the party Possum went to the place where all the animals had gathered for the dance and found the best seat for himself. When it came time for him to dance he loosened the string from his tail and walked to the middle of the dance floor and all the animals made a circle around him.

"Possum began to sing loudly about his beautiful tail, dancing around and bragging.

"'See how beautiful the fur is,'" he sang, and danced.

"All the animals watching him began laughing and pointing to his tail.

"Possum kept dancing and singing while the animals continued to laugh loudly. Possum looked around the circle and saw that all the animals were laughing and pointing to his tail. Then he looked over his shoulder at his tail and saw that it was bare with not a hair left on it. He was so embarrassed and ashamed that he could not say a word. He just rolled over on the ground and played dead.

"Now to this day Possum will roll over and play dead if he thinks he's in danger."

Janie hooted with laughter. She couldn't wait to hear more of Old Jess's stories.

"Grandmother was right," Janie thought. "He is a wonderful storyteller."

Old Jess looked at Janie and smiled.

"What a wonderful story, Old Jess," Janie said, returning his smile. "Thank you for sharing it with me."

The two friends remained by the river's edge enjoying being with each other and the afternoon passed quickly.

"I am enjoying our visit, but it's beginning to get dark. Shouldn't you start back to your cabin now?"

"I can find my cabin in the dark," he assured Janie.

"You can?"

"Yes. I can go anywhere in the dark."

"Without a light?" Janie asked.

Old Jess nodded, grinning at Janie.

"Why, when I was a young man I'd walk about ten miles to a girl's house from where I lived with my family. I'd visit with her for a while and then walk back home in the dark."

"You're kidding me," Janie laughed.

"No, it's true," he answered with a broad smile on his face.

"You would go see her, and then walk back home? A twenty mile round trip? At night? Without any kind of light?"

"Sure," Old Jess answered, chuckling to himself. "I liked that girl."

Janie laughed, and wondered if he was teasing her.

"And there were many nights when my daddy and I would walk to the river from our cabin and fish in the dark."

Janie shook her head from side to side, giggling at the thought of someone fishing at night without a light.

"So you see, as long as I know where I'm going, walking in the dark doesn't bother me."

"You're amazing," Janie said.

"Like I said, I can go anywhere in the dark," he said proudly.

"I repeat it," Janie laughed. "You are just amazing!"

"Janie, the dark won't harm you...it is not to be feared. Learn to listen. Night sounds are wonderful. They speak to the soul."

"You are so wise, my friend. I am glad you decided to visit me."

Old Jess smiled at Janie affectionately as he prepared to leave. And then...he was gone...silently...as usual...with a wave over his shoulder, and Janie was left with new wonders about her old friend. She could hardly wait for his next visit. This time she would ask if she could paint him.

CHAPTER THIRTY-THREE

*J*anie stood at the window in her living room and stared at the river for a moment. Then her gaze swept upward toward the cloudless blue sky.

"What a beautiful day," she thought.

When she looked toward the water again a movement on the other side of the river caught her eye. She saw something at the water's edge and, straining to get a better look, she pressed her face close to the window pane, thinking that it might be Old Jess.

"There it is again," she whispered aloud. "An animal! It's some kind of animal...a very large animal."

She turned away from the window and hurried to get her binoculars.

"I don't think it's a deer," she thought as she rushed back to the window. "It could be a very large dog."

Lifting the binoculars to her eyes she saw the animal running into the woods, leaving her disappointed that she had not gotten a better look at it.

"Maybe it will come back," she thought, lowering the binoculars from her eyes. Janie pulled a chair close to the window, sat down and stared out the window.

After waiting for almost an hour, she stood and sighed, "I thought the animal might return to the river. Maybe tomorrow I'll see it again."

The next morning Janie was sitting on her porch when she saw the animal again. She got her binoculars and looked toward the river. She couldn't see it clearly as it was half hidden behind a large rock so she decided to go out in the yard and walk quietly down toward the river to try to gain a better look.

She had moved only a few steps when the animal sensed her presence and it turned and ran into the woods.

"I think that might be a coyote," Janie thought while she walked back to her house.

Several days passed and Janie continued to look for the animal each time she gazed at the river, but she had not seen it again.

One afternoon while she was planting a Cherokee Rose bush in her front yard she glanced toward the water and saw Old Jess approaching the river.

"I'll be right there," she called loudly, waving to him, always glad to see her new friend.

She ran into the house for a moment, got a small box and then hurried down to the river to visit with Old Jess.

He was sitting on the grass and Janie lowered herself down beside him.

Old Jess reached into his pocket. "I made something for you,"

Janie's face showed surprise. "For me?"

"Yes."

"This is a corn bead necklace," he said, handing the necklace to her.

"It's beautiful. Thank you," Janie said. "You made this?"

Old Jess nodded.

"The beads are beautiful." Janie said, fingering the beads.

"They come from a plant called the medicine bead or Job's Tears. The plants grow tall all summer and drop their seeds in the fall. They are very strong, and will grow even if they are not cultivated."

"Really?" Janie said, while she looked at the gray-colored beads in the necklace.

Old Jess chuckled and nodded. "One time they took over my entire garden."

Janie looked up in surprise.

"There is a story among our people about these beads."

"Is it one that you can tell to me, Old Jess?"

"Yes. The story goes that at the time when the soldiers drove our people west on the Trail of Tears the tall plant of the corn beads began to grow where our people wept."

"Oh," Janie said sadly,

"I like the necklace you are wearing," Old Jess said, pointing to the turquoise stone Janie wore.

"Thank you," Janie replied, her hand moving to touch the nugget while she slipped the corn bead necklace around her neck. "It belonged to my father."

"It's pretty," Old Jess smiled.

"Now, I have something I want to show you," Janie said, picking up the small box. "I remembered to bring it today."

Old Jess glanced at the box, and then leaned toward Janie, smiling.

"Look," she said, pulling the wooden turtle out of the box. "I want you to see this," she added, handing the carving to the old man.

"Oh," Old Jess exclaimed, taking the turtle and turning it over and over in his hands, noting every detail. "This is good work."

"Yes, it's beautiful, isn't it?" responded Janie. "Jim gave it to me when I first moved here."

Old Jess nodded.

"It's carved from the wood of a Yellow Poplar Tree," Janie said.

"The Tulip Tree," Old Jess said, nodding his head slowly.

"Jim carved it himself"

"The doctor carved it?" Old Jess asked, glancing at Janie.

"Yes," she smiled, nodding, " I'm very proud of it."

"It's good work," the old man repeated. "Did he tell you what the designs mean?"

"No, and I didn't think to ask him. I just thought it was very beautiful."

"Would you like to know their meanings?"

"Oh, very much!" Janie exclaimed. "Please tell me."

Old Jess looked closely at the intricate designs

and began turning the turtle in his hands as he point-
ed to each clan. "The outer edge of the shell has the
masks of the seven Cherokee clans. See, here are the
Deer Clan, the Long Hair Clan, the Paint Clan, the
Bird Clan, the Blue Clan, the Deer Clan and the Wild
Potato Clan."

After he finished telling Janie the meaning of each
design he handed the carving back to her with a gleam
in his eye.

Janie knew the old man and recognized the look.

"What mischievousness are you thinking up
now?" she asked with a grin.

"Oh, nothing," he answered, "nothing at all."

Old Jess had seen one other design on the turtle
he had not mentioned, but he knew what the good
doctor had in mind when he added that image. He
had noticed a tiny Cherokee Wedding Vase had been
carefully carved in the middle of the turtle's head.

"Come on, tell me," Janie urged.

"No, not today," he said, shaking his head as he
handed the carving back to Janie.

Janie put the turtle back in the box and moved
closer to Old Jess.

"There's something I want to ask you." she said.

When Janie finished telling him about her sight-
ings of the animal, Old Jess agreed with her, thinking
also that the animal was probably a coyote.

"He will probably come back again. Do you have a
camera?"

"Yes,"

"See if you can get a picture of him," Old Jess suggested.

"That's a good idea," Janie said. "I will."

Since Janie's paintings were mostly landscapes
and flowers she wanted to try something new.

"I would like to paint this animal if I can get a
closer look. If I put out some food," she thought,
"maybe it will return."

CHAPTER THIRTY-FOUR

*J*anie went to the river bank almost every day anxiously scanning the woods around the water, hoping to get a glimpse of the animal again. She had seen it briefly the day before at the river's edge drinking water and had grabbed her camera and hurried down the cabin steps. When the animal spotted Janie it had raised its head and stared straight at her for a moment. Then it darted away. Janie watched as the animal vanished among the foliage on the other side of the river. This time she had gotten a better look and thought that the animal might be a wolf. While she walked on to the river she thought about her pet wolf, Wa-Yah.

"I wonder what happened to him," she mused softly. "I guess I'll never know."

Janie gazed across the river at the dense thicket of laurel swaying in the gentle wind. The breeze moved through the leaves on the nearby trees, and washed over her face with its coolness.

"I wish the wolf would come back now," she whispered while she sat down in the soft grass.

Sighing, she stretched out on the grass and looked up at the cloudless blue sky. Her eyes grew heavy as she stared upward and she fell asleep almost immediately.

She had slept a short time when she awoke with a start. A noise had alerted her senses and she sat up and looked around. She saw nothing unusual except for the change in the sky since she had been asleep. It was filled with dark rain clouds.

A sudden clap of thunder pierced the air.

"Oh, so that's what woke me..." she smiled, looking up, " ...thunder."

A raindrop fell on Janie's face followed by another crash of thunder.

She jumped up and ran for the cabin while the rain began to fall heavily. By the time she reached her home her clothes and hair were soaked.

The telephone was ringing when she entered the cabin. She hurried to get a towel and then rushed to the phone.

"Hello," she said, rubbing the towel over her wet hair.

"Hello. I've just landed at the airport and I went straight to the phone to call you."

Janie smiled.

Jim had been away for a week and she was anxious to see him, however, she dreaded telling him about a recent decision she had made.

"I've missed you," Jim said.

"And I've missed you," Janie replied.

"Would it be all right if I come down to see you tonight?"

"Certainly," answered Janie. "I'll cook dinner for us."

"Great!" I'll be there around six o'clock"

Janie hung up the phone and hesitated before she pulled the towel over her hair again.

"How am I going to tell him?" she wondered, walking to the window and gazing out into the yard at the flowers she had planted.

CHAPTER THIRTY-FIVE

$\mathcal{L}$ater that afternoon Janie settled herself in a chair on the cabin deck and called Millie, anxious to tell her friend about her recent decision ...a decision that had been hard to make, but one Janie felt was necessary.

"Hi, Millie. What are you doing?" Janie asked.

"Nothing much, just resting after a long shift at the hospital. How about you?"

"I'm fine. Listen, I called to tell you some news."

"What?" Millie asked eagerly.

"I'm going out west for a while."

"You're going where?" Millie asked, surprised.

"Out west," Janie said, raising her voice.

"Really?"

"Yes." Janie confirmed.

"Why the sudden urge to travel?"

"I've decided to go to Oklahoma to see if I can find any of Mother and Daddy's relatives."

"How long will you be gone?"

"I don't know. I suppose there's no rush to get back."

"No?"

"Well, since Emily got married and moved away she seldom comes back here to visit and Hunter is at the art gallery in New Mexico," Janie rushed through her explanation to Millie. "I plan to visit him while I'm out there."

"Janie," Millie said seriously, "what about Jim?"

"Well..." Janie paused.

"Have you told him?"

"No," Janie responded softly. "He's coming tonight and I'll tell him."

142

"What's wrong, Janie? Have you and Jim had an argument?" Millie asked seriously.

"No...in fact, just the opposite." Janie answered.

"What do you mean?"

"Millie, I think that he's close to proposing marriage to me."

"That's great! I'm not surprised."

Janie didn't respond.

"So what's the problem?" Millie pushed for an answer.

Janie remained silent for a moment, then spoke softly. "I'm not sure I'm ready for marriage."

"Do you love Jim?" Millie asked.

"Yes," Janie said softly. "I love him."

"Well, girl, what's wrong with you? You two are perfect for each other."

Janie didn't respond.

"Are you really going away, Janie?" Millie asked seriously.

"Yes. Do you want to go with me?"

"I wish I could, but...work, you know."

"I understand."

"When are you leaving?"

"Well, I want to spend some time with Grandmother before I leave, and I want to see you also."

"So when are you leaving?" Millie repeated.

"I'm not sure. I'll call you before I come to Ashville."

"Call me tonight after Jim leaves," Millie said. She hung up the phone slowly, wondering about Janie's sudden decision to leave...and also why her friend was running away from Jim...if she loved him.

CHAPTER THIRTY-SIX

*J*anie stood leaning on the porch railing gazing toward the river while she waited for Jim to arrive. She listened to the water as it rushed over the rocks on its way down the river. She never tired of hearing it. To her the river sounded like a beautiful melodic aria.

Janie knew the early cool days of fall would soon arrive bringing with them the colorful leaves decorating the trees, but today was warm so she had decided to serve their meal on the back deck.

Glancing toward the road she saw Jim's car approaching and she ran to the top of the stairs to wait for him. He had been out of town for over a week and she had missed him and was anxious to be with him again.

Jim jumped out of the car and leaped up the porch stairs taking two at a time. He gathered Janie into his arms and hugged her tightly.

"I am so glad to see you," he said. "I've missed you so much."

Before Janie had a chance to respond, he kissed her, his lips lingering on her mouth. The kiss was unsettling and Janie's response was immediate. She returned the kiss with ardor and let out a long sigh when it ended, smiling at Jim. Telling him was going to be harder than she thought, but now, even more so, she had to leave.

Janie sat staring at the flickering flame of the candle on the table after they finished eating. Then her gaze moved to watch the fireflies flashing in the air around the cabin. She had dreaded this moment all day and had avoided looking directly at Jim during the meal, afraid that her eyes would betray her worry. She had antagonized over her relationship with him for weeks. They had been dating for over a year and their feelings for each other had deepened. Recently Jim had hinted marriage to Janie. She had smiled and quickly changed the subject. Janie frowned, knowing that she must tell him of her plans tonight and she wasn't sure how he would react.

"Would you like more coffee?" she asked.

"No, thank you," he replied with a smile. "The dinner was delicious, Janie."

"I'm glad you enjoyed it," she responded with a smile.

"By the way, would you like to see a Cherokee Stick Ball Game?"

"I would love it," Janie said enthusiastically, leaning slightly toward Jim.

"A game is going to be played at the Cherokee Fall Festival on Saturday. I'll come and pick you up and we will go,"

"Thank you," Janie replied, smiling back at him. She took a deep breath, put her hands in her lap and clasped them tightly together.

"Jim, there's something I need to tell you," she began, her gaze moving to look into his eyes.

"And what is that?" he smiled, his eyes crinkling.

"You know that I care deeply for you, Jim, don't you?" Janie said.

"I love you, Janie," he replied seriously.

"And I love you," she replied, bringing her hand up to touch his cheek, then placing it back in her lap.

"So what do you want to tell me?" he asked.

Janie hesitated before speaking. "I'm going away for a while..." she answered bluntly, "...out west."

"What?"

"I'm going away," she repeated.

"Away?"

Janie nodded.

"Yes, I'm going to be gone for a while," she said.

"For how long?" Jim asked, clearly surprised at her decision.

"I'm not sure," she answered, almost in a whisper.

"But, you are coming back, aren't you?" Jim asked, anxiously waiting her reply, leaning toward her and grasping both her hands.

Janie could see the concern in his eyes.

"Yes," she said, smiling, patting his hand. "Yes, I'm coming back."

And to lighten the mood, she added with a grin, "You're not getting rid of me forever."

"Thank goodness!" he sighed, leaned back in his chair and relaxed.

"But, I really don't know how long I'll be gone. I want to visit Hunter in New Mexico...and maybe try to find where my grandparents are buried in Oklahoma."

Jim nodded.

"Grandmother Rose would like to know where their graves are located," Janie words rushed on.

Janie wanted to be honest with Jim. She knew that the words she had spoken were true, but she couldn't tell him the real reason for the trip.

"You know I'll miss you and..." Jim said.

Janie interrupted. "I'll miss you too,but I must go."

"I understand. Would you like for me to fly you out there?"

Janie hesitated and then responded slowly. "That would be nice, but can you take the time away from your work?"

"I'll make the time," he answered, smiling at Janie. "When do you want to go?"

"I would like to visit Grandmother and Millie before I leave, but whenever it's convenient for you will be fine."

"I'll look at my schedule when I get back to the hospital," he replied.

"Thank you, Jim."

Jim stood, took Janie's hand as she rose from the chair and pulled her into his arms. Cupping her face in his hands he kissed her. The kiss was long and Janie could feel her heart beating rapidly.

"I love you so much," Jim said hoarsely, gently

pushing her away to look into her eyes.

Before she could respond he pulled her tightly against him and his lips touched her cheek and then met her mouth again.

Janie could feel his heart pounding wildly against her own racing heart as their bodies pressed against each other.

When the kiss ended Jim stepped back from Janie, and smiled.

"Look," he said, motioning toward the sky.

The full yellow moon was gradually rising from behind the distant mountains. Its light cast a soft glow across the river and over the yard.

"Oh," Janie exclaimed, "it's beautiful, isn't it?"

"Yes, but not as beautiful as you are, Janie, my darling."

He gathered her closely into his arms again and pressed his mouth against her lips.

Late that night after Jim left to return to Ashville Janie went immediately to the telephone and called Millie.

"Millie! I told him!" Janie blurted out as soon as her friend answered the phone.

"You told Jim you are going out west?"

"Yes."

"Did you tell him the main reason you are going?" Millie asked, wishing that Janie would tell him the true reason for the trip.

"No," Janie answered softly.

There was silence between the two women for a moment, then Janie's words rushed on.

"He's going to fly me to Santa Fe in his airplane," Janie said.

"Lucky you!" Millie said.

Millie knew her friend well by now. She knew Janie was not making the trip just for the reasons her friend had told her. Millie had sensed that it had more to do with Janie's feelings for Jim than she was willing to discuss.

Millie and Hunter, now becoming very good friends, talked on the phone about this often and both of them agreed that it would be good for her to be with Jim. And they hoped that Janie would soon find the peace she sought so she could open her heart to accept the happiness she deserved.

CHAPTER THIRTY-SEVEN

*T*wo days later Janie and Jim attended the Cherokee Stick Ball Game and Janie was surprised when she saw Old Jess on the stage announcing the game plays.

"Old Jess never stops amazing me," Janie told Jim, shaking her head and laughing.

"Do you know Old Jess?" Jim asked, surprised.

"Oh, yes. We are old friends. I thought I had told you about meeting him at the river."

"No," Jim answered.

"Do you know him?" Janie asked.

"Yes. He's one of our most respected elders."

"I really like him," Janie assured Jim. "He's been a good friend to me."

The next day and the following day Janie did not see Old Jess at the river, but within a week he was back.

Janie waited while she watched the old man slowly approach their usual meeting place.

"I've missed you," she smiled.

"I saw you and the doctor at the game," he began as soon as he sat down beside Janie. "Did you like the game?"

"Oh, yes, I did, but it was rough! I'm surprised someone didn't get hurt," Janie said.

"The men were all good players," Old Jess said, nodding his head.

"I enjoyed hearing your comments during the game," Janie said, smiling at the old man. "Have you ever played the game?"

"Yes, many times...when I was younger," he

added, smiling.

Janie returned Old Jess' smile.

"Did you know that our stick ball is the oldest ball game in America?"

Janie nodded. "Yes, I have heard that it is."

"I like the old Cherokee story about the game's very beginning when the animals and birds had ball teams and played each other," Old Jess said.

"Please, tell me the story," Janie said enthusiastically, moving closer to the old man. "I love the Cherokee stories."

Old Jess smiled, pleased that Janie was interested in the story. He moved to a nearby tree, sat down, settled himself with his back resting against the tree trunk, and patted the grass for Janie to join him. When they were settled he cleared his throat and began the story.

"Well," he said, "there were two teams. The bear was the captain for the animals and the eagle was captain for the fowl of the air. The bear's team consisted of panther, wolf, bobcat, deer, boar and many other strong animals. The eagle's team had all kinds of flying birds on it.One day, as the teams were getting ready to play a game, a little mouse came along and asked the bear if he could play on his team.

"'You are so little,' the bear said. 'What do you think you could do?' Then he kicked the little mouse and the little mouse went sailing through the air. He got up and shook himself off while the big bear watched and laughed.

"Then the little mouse went to see Captain Eagle and asked it he could join his team.

"And the eagle said, 'Sure, we welcome you.'

"'But, I can't fly', the little mouse told the eagle.

"'That's no problem,' the eagle said.

"Then the eagle looked all around and found something to use to make the little mouse a pair of wings and he put it on the mouse so he could fly. When the game got underway, before the ball ever fell to the ground, the little mouse grabbed it, flapped his little wings fast and scored. From then on the little mouse dominated the game, making point after point, and the eagle's team won the game over the bear that had made fun of him."

"Oh...I think..." Janie began.

"Now, the moral of that story is this," Old Jess interrupted. "Don't ever underestimate the size of a person, or their looks or the color of their skin when they want to join your team, your school, your church, or your community. Always welcome them in or they just might win over you," Old Jess smiled as he finished the story.

"What a wonderful story," Janie said, softly clapping her hands.

"Now," Old Jess said, "if you look up in the sky about dusk you might see him flying around. Do you know what he is?"

Janie hesitated and then asked in surprise, "A bat?"

"Yes!" Old Jess chuckled, pleased Janie knew the answer.

CHAPTER THIRTY-EIGHT

*J*anie had completed all her plans for the trip. Her luggage was packed and reservations were made at the hotel where she would be staying in Santa Fe. She had visited her grandmother and would go to Millie's house tomorrow. Before she left the mountains, she wanted to take one last hike in the woods to see the leaves beginning to turn the fall colors. She took her hiking stick and headed out of the cabin, thinking that the warm day with a cloudless blue sky was perfect for her walk.

When Janie returned to her usual resting place by the river after her walk she was very tired. Leaning back on a tree she stood for a moment, wiped her brow and then sat down in the grassy area around the tree. She closed her eyes and the sound of the rushing water and the feel of the warm sunshine on her body lulled Janie into a light sleep almost immediately.

She had not dozed long when she felt something touch her body. She lay still and when she felt it again her hand moved slowly to her side. She felt hair. She quickly drew her hand back and cautiously opened her eyes. When she turned to look beside her she gasped and covered her mouth to silence a scream! Her breath came rapidly and her heart beat wildly!

Lying close to her body was an animal.

Blinking her eyes she focused on it and thought that the animal was the one she had seen at the water. Apparently it had walked up and lain down beside her. Strangely Janie felt no fear of the black and gray animal lying beside her. Leaning over slightly to gain a closer look at it she caught her breath!

It was a wolf...the wolf she had seen in the woods earlier!

"Wa-Yah," she whispered softly, thinking of her long lost pet.

Suddenly the wolf raised its head and looked straight into Janie's eyes.

"Can this be Wa-Yah?" she wondered, looking closely at the animal's color and markings.

Yes! She was sure that it was Wa-Yah!

Janie eased her hand up slowly and touched the top of the wolf's head.

"You are Wa-Yah.. I know you are," she whispered, with tears of joy in her eyes. "You are not dead."

The wolf did not move and continued to stare at Janie.

"I've found you! No, you found me! I thought I would never see you again," she whispered, resisting the urge to throw her arms around the wolf and hug it tightly like she had done so many times before with Wa-Yah.

Suddenly the wolf sprang to its feet, looked at Janie and then quickly ran toward the woods, never looking back.

Janie jumped to her feet.

"Wa-Yah! Wa-Yah!" she called watching the animal speed away.

She ran, trying to catch up with the wolf, but it was too fast for her. She stopped at the edge of the woods, and watched as it disappeared into the thicket.

"Oh, please, come back!" she called. "Please, come back!"

Janie sank down on the ground and stayed by the river for over an hour, hoping the wolf would return, but she saw no sign of it. Finally she walked toward her cabin, often turning to look back at the place where the animal had disappeared.

She walked slowly up the cabin steps and onto the porch, while glancing at the woods around the river. She moved to the front of the porch and stood at the railing thinking about what had happened. She wondered if she had dreamed about the animal.

"No!" she said aloud, shaking her head. "It was no dream. That was Wa-Yah! I know it was him! I know it was him! He will come back! I just know he will!"

Janie looked up and saw that a beautiful rainbow had appeared in the sky...and suddenly remembered Grandmother Rose had told her many times she would have a sign guiding her path. Could this rainbow be a sign of good things to come?

"Is this really a sign?" she pondered as she entered her home to begin the final preparations for her trip. "Did she dare have hope?"

Janie had much to consider...for she had learned at an early age to believe in her grandmother's teachings.

CHAPTER THIRTY-NINE

*E*arly the next morning, as she did so often, Janie stood at the window drinking her first cup of coffee of the day while she looked at the river. She yawned, put her cup down on the table, stretched her arms over her head and yawned again. She had not slept well and she was tired. She had tossed and turned in the bed all night while her thoughts were torn between leaving on her trip and staying home to try to see the wolf again.

"I have to go," she whispered aloud, picking up her coffee cup. "I need to decide how I will answer Jim. I know I love him, but do I love him enough to marry him?" She shook her head. "I don't know. I just don't know."

She remembered Jim had told her he wanted to ask her a very important question after she returned from the west. She had smiled at him but had not responded. Now she needed to know the answer. She thought being away from him would help her make the decision.

She glanced down at the river again and saw Old Jess had come and she waved to him.

Hurrying into the kitchen she picked up a container of strawberries for them to eat while they visited.

"So you are going away from the doctor," Old Jess said as soon as Janie sat down beside him. He wondered if they had a misunderstanding. Could that be the reason for her leaving?

"Well, yes, for a while," Janie responded.

"You two are good together," Old Jess said. "You should be married."

Janie remained silent.

Picking up a strawberry Old Jess motioned to it and said, "Do you want to hear a story?"

Janie nodded eagerly and smiled at Old Jess. She loved to hear his stories.

"This is a Cherokee story about what happened one day to the first man and first woman. There are several versions of this story, but I am going to tell you the one I like."

Janie moved closer to the old man and settled herself, ready to listen to his deep voice.

"Long ago when the world was new the Creator made a man and a woman. He didn't want them to be lonely so he made them at the same time. They married and for a long time they lived together and were happy. But one day the man came home from hunting and was hungry and wanted to eat, but the wife had not prepared anything for their meal. Instead she was outside picking flowers. Now, this made the man angry with her and he stared shouting, calling her names.

"'Look at these beautiful flowers I picked. I thought you would like them,' the woman said.

"'I am hungry. I can't eat flowers,' he snapped.

"The wife's feelings were hurt and she burst into tears. Then she became angry too.

"'Your words hurt me. I will not live with you any longer,' she said as she ran out of the house and began walking toward the sun in the west.

"When she didn't come back the husband got worried so he tried to find her. He followed, but her steps were quick and he couldn't keep up with her. He was fast but she was faster.

"The sun watched as the man hurried along and saw that the husband was sorry he had hurt his wife's feelings and the sun took pity on him. The sun asked the man it he was still angry with his wife and the man shook his head.

"'No,' he said. 'I should not have spoken angry words to my wife. I want to tell her, but I can not catch up with her to tell her I am sorry. She is too fast for me.'

"'Then I will help you,' offered the sun."

Old Jess paused for a moment and took a bite of the strawberry he held in his hand, then continued.

"The sun shone down in front of the woman and everywhere it touched the ground strawberries grew. They were bright red and the woman stopped when she saw them in front of her. She knelt down and picked one of them and bit into it. She had never tasted anything like it before. It was very sweet and it reminded her of how happy she and her husband had been together before they quarreled.

"'I will go back and take him some of these strawberries,' she thought. And while she was picking the berries the man caught up with her.

"'I am sorry for my ugly words to you. Please forgive me,' he said to his wife.

"She answered him by giving him some of the strawberries to share their sweetness and they became happy once again."

Old Jess smiled and then took another bite of the strawberry.

"What a beautiful story," Janie said.

"And today when the Cherokee people eat strawberries they are reminded to always be kind to each other and remember that respect and friendship are as sweet as the ripe red berries," Old Jess said.

"I will never forget that story, Old Jess," Janie promised.

"Now, I must go," Old Jess said, rising to his feet. "I will see you when you return."

Janie stood. "I will miss you," she said, hugging the old man. "Take care of yourself while I'm gone."

"You hurry back to the doctor," Old Jess said with a grin.

She watched the old man cross the river, and then waved before he disappeared into the woods.

"I wish I could see Wa-Yah before I leave," Janie thought as she walked back to her cabin. "I know that was Wa-Yah I saw at the river."

While she dressed and prepared to leave, she continued going to the window often, hoping to get a look at the wolf once more.

When she got into her car and drove away she did not realize that a pair of blue eyes was watching her. Standing in the shadows of the trees near the cabin the wolf watched the car until it disappeared down the mountain. Then it turned slowly and went back into the nearby woods.

Janie enjoyed her overnight visit with Millie and Jim picked her up early the next morning to take her to the airport to begin their trip.

The day had dawned with plenty of sunshine and a beautiful clear blue sky.

"Perfect for flying," Jim commented, glancing at the sky as he helped Janie into his airplane.

She sat in the seat beside Jim and watched him carefully maneuver the plane down the runway and into the air

Jim turned to her and smiled. "We have a perfect day for our trip."

Janie returned his smile.

As she watched the scenery on the ground below Janie continued to think about Jim, knowing she loved him. But marriage? She wasn't sure she wanted to be married again. She hoped while she was away the distance between them would help her make the important decision.

"I must be prepared with an answer," she thought, wondering how she would respond when the time came.

She loved Jim too much to hurt him and she knew Jim loved her. They had both suffered losses and neither of them needed more heartache. She must make the right decision for both of them.

CHAPTER FORTY

*A*nother beautiful day for flying," Jim thought while his airplane soared into the air and left Santa Fe.

The return flight had been easy and uneventful until Jim reached Tennessee. The heavens became darker as dusk approached. Suddenly it began to rain lightly and then continued into a steady downpour.

Jim could hardly see beyond the window of the plane while the wipers flapped wildly at high speed trying to move the water away from the windshield. He frowned, hoping to get out of the bad weather soon. But the torrential rains continued and he leaned forward in an attempt to gain better vision in front of him.

Suddenly the plane's engine began to make a strange noise. Jim glanced at the gauges in front of him and nothing appeared unusual. But when the plane began to vibrate Jim knew that he was in trouble. He contacted the nearest airport and reported the problem, hoping for directions to the nearest landing site. After the location was given, static suddenly developed on the speaker and Jim lost contact with the control tower.

The airplane began to descend slowly and then steadily toward the ground while Jim tried to bring it back up. Realizing that it was not possible his thoughts then were to attempt to land the plane, but he couldn't see through the rain and had no radio contact for help.

Jim knew there was no time to try to bail out of the plane when he heard the plane's wings snapping tree limbs on its journey to the ground.

Suddenly the airplane bounced rapidly touching land, and then...darkness everywhere...and only the pounding rain broke the silence.

Janie smiled as she drove through the streets of Santa Fe remembering the night before with Jim. She had gone to the airport with him and watched while his plane flew into the air for its return trip to Ashville. She had rented a car at the airport and was now on her way to visit Hunter when her cell phone rang.

"Hello," she answered happily.

"Janie, I..."

"Millie! Oh, let me tell you...the flight out here was beautiful and..."

"Janie..." Millie interrupted.

"Millie, Jim and I went to the most wonderful restaurant for dinner last night and then..."

"Janie," Millie broke in again.

"We rode around the city and, Millie, it's so beautiful out here," Janie's voice raced on. "And then we ..."

Millie raised her voice, "Janie! Listen!"

"Let me tell you that Jim..." Janie continued.

"Janie! Stop!" Millie demanded sharply. "Listen to me! It's important!"

"What is it?"

"Are you driving?" Millie asked.

"Yes. I rented a car and am on my way to do some shopping and then go to see Hunter."

"Pull off the road and park."

"What?"

"Pull off the road and park."

"You sound serious," Janie said, while she slowed the car and moved to the roadside.

"I am. Janie, something's happened...something bad."

"What is it?" Janie asked, thinking about her grandmother.

There was silence for a moment.

"Janie, it's Jim."

"Jim?"

"Yes."

"What about him?"

Millie took a deep breath and continued.

"Janie, Jim didn't get back to Ashville."

"What do you mean?" Janie asked.

"I hate to tell you this, Janie," Millie began, "but Jim's plane is missing."

"What? What did you say?" panic rising in Janie's voice.

"His plane is missing."

"Are you sure?"

"Yes."

Tears sprang to Janie's eyes. This couldn't be happening to her again.

"What happened?" Janie asked, her voice breaking.

"The weather was bad and the control tower lost contact with him. Before the radio stopped working Jim told them something was wrong with the engine and the plane was descending fast. Then there was a lot of static on the radio and they lost contact with him. The search parties are in the area, but they haven't located the plane yet."

Millie could hear Janie's sobs.

"Oh, Janie, I'm so sorry to tell you all of this, but I thought you should know," Millie said and then added, "I wish I were there with you."

Tears poured from Janie's eyes and down her cheeks. She couldn't speak.

"Janie?"

Janie did not respond.

"Janie, answer me!" Millie said, loudly. "Are you all right?"

"No!" Janie answered, and then added, "I'm not all right! Millie, I love him!"

"Yes, I know," Millie said quietly.

"I'm coming home...as soon as I can get a flight," Janie said, wiping tears with the back of her hand.

"Call me. I'll meet you at the airport," Millie said.

Sitting in the airplane on the return trip to

Ashville Janie's body felt numb from the shock of learning of Jim's disappearance. She had prayed constantly for Jim's safety. He couldn't leave her too. She knew now that the question that had plagued her for weeks was answered. The decision was made.

"I will never leave him again," she vowed silently. "I want him by my side forever...as my husband. If only it's not too late...."

She closed her eyes and leaned back in the seat while silent tears ran down her cheeks. Her thoughts raced over all the events of her life as she drifted into a disturbed, restless sleep.

CHAPTER FORTY-ONE

Months later...

"It's a beautiful day. Would all of you like to go out and sit on the porch?" Janie asked her guests after they finished eating.

Everyone agreed and stood to leave the table.

Janie noticed that Hunter and Millie were the first to stand. She watched as they hurried out on the porch, knowing that they wanted to claim the swing for themselves so they could sit close to each other. When they sat down Janie saw Hunter whisper something to Millie and take her hand. She was happy that they were a couple now and hoped that there would be a wedding in their future.

Rose, Tara, Steve, Emily and Emily's husband, Brad, followed Janie outside, all commenting on the delicious meal.

"I loved the bean bread," Tara said.

"And the pumpkin bread was delicious," added Emily.

"How about the chestnut bread?" Steve asked. "Wasn't that good?"

"I liked the Indian tacos the best!" Brad chimed in "The fry bread was really good!"

"I liked it all!" Hunter said, laughing, patting his stomach.

Janie was pleased her guests had enjoyed the Indian food she had prepared for lunch.

When they were settled, Janie walked to the porch railing and looked out at the river. She was glad she had selected the perfect setting for her home. The yard was arrayed with flowers of all the colors of spring and the sights offered a huge variety of scenes for her paintings. She thought about the many beautiful canvasses she had stored in her home and was thinking about opening a small gallery for selling them. She remembered that when she told Old Jess about her idea he had been excited and offered to contribute a few of his carvings for the gallery. Rose and Tara were working on quilted samplers which could be sold in the gallery also. Everyone was encouraging her, especially Hunter. He had commented that he might be her partner. She knew that would make Millie happy.

Turning to face everyone she took a deep breath and leaned back on the railing.

"It pleases me that all of you are here and will take part in the service," she said, gazing at her friends and family.

"We're glad we're here too," Emily said, smiling at her sister.

The others nodded in agreement.

"Tell us about the plans for the ceremony, Janie," Millie inquired.

"Well," she began, "it will be a traditional Cherokee ceremony conducted by Old Jess."

She paused and took another deep breath, thinking about the events to come. She wanted everything to be perfect and had spent hours in the planning.

"It sounds lovely," Millie said.

Everyone was quiet for a moment.

"I wish Jim was here," Hunter said, breaking the silence.

"I do too," Janie responded. "I miss him."

"It was a miracle he survived the plane crash," Rose said softly.

"Yes, it was," Millie agreed.

"His minor injuries healed quickly, but the broken leg is taking a little longer. He's better now, but he still walks with a limp," Janie explained. "That will go away with time. He's improving every day. His leg doesn't slow him down at all."

"Can't keep a good man down," laughed Steve.

"That's right," Brad agreed.

"Does he know about all these wedding plans?" Hunter teased.

"Hunter!" scolded Millie, as she playfully punched his arm.

"Oh yes!" Janie laughed. "We've discussed them over and over."

"Well, all right," Hunter joked. "Just checking. All of you remember that I haven't been back from Santa Fe too long so I'm behind with all the news. I'm just trying to catch up."

Everyone laughed.

"I'm anxious to meet my soon to be brother-in-law," Emily said.

"Jim's out of town performing surgery," Janie explained, "but he'll be back in time for the wedding, I assure you!" Janie laughed.

"That's good," Hunter said, and everyone joined in the good humor.

Janie smiled fondly at her brother. She was glad he moved to Ashville when he left Santa Fe. They had talked for hours after he arrived and Hunter had told her about his relationship with Millie. "I'm in love with her, Janie," he had said seriously.

"So that's why you moved to Ashville," Janie had said playfully.

"Yep!" he responded.

Janie was delighted at the news.

"Where are you going for the honeymoon?" Emily asked.

"Now, that's a secret," Janie giggled. "I can't tell you!"

"Come on, Sis, fess up," Hunter teased, determined to find out about all of the wedding news. "Where are you and Jim going?"

"You'll have to ask Jim," Janie responded, determined not to reveal their secret.

"Where are you and Jim going to live when you return from the honeymoon?" Hunter pushed on with his questions.

"We plan to live in Jim's house in Ashville and in

the cabin. When he's out of town I'll probably come back to the cabin for a few days. When he has the time we'll both come here," she explained, pleased that she and Jim had decided on this arrangement.

"Sounds good to me," Hunter remarked with a satisfied smile.

"I'm enjoying this visit with everyone, but now I think it's time for all of us to leave after we clean up the kitchen," Rose said. "I know Janie has much to do before the wedding."

"I'll stay and help Janie clean up," offered Millie, rising from the swing.

"I'll help too," Hunter said, quickly standing and looking at Millie.

"Oh, you just want to stay with Millie," Emily teased good-naturedly.

"You got that right, Sis!" Hunter responded, grinning broadly at Millie who returned his smile.

"Do you think there's going to be another wedding soon?" Brad whispered to Emily.

"Who knows?" Emily answered, then added when she glanced at Hunter and noticed that he had his arm around Millie, "I wouldn't be surprised."

Rose looked at her grandchildren and smiled wishfully. "How wonderful it is that we are all together for this happy occasion," she thought. "I wish Lone Wolf was here. He would have enjoyed seeing his grandchildren all grown-up and happy."

As they stood to leave Steve hurried to the deck railing. "Look! Down at the river!"

Everyone followed Steve to have a look.

"Oh, it's Wa-Yah," Janie explained. "He comes to the river almost every day now. I usually join him for a visit and sometimes he walks with me when I hike."

"He's beautiful," Emily said. "I wish he'd come closer."

"He comes up to the cabin occasionally," Janie explained.

As quickly as Wa-Yah appeared he turned and disappeared.

"Oh, he's gone," Emily said with disappointment

in her voice.

"Come on, everybody, let's get out of Janie's way," Tara said, "I know she has a lot to do to."

Later after everyone had gone Janie was sitting in her living room going over the last minute plans for the wedding when she heard a scratching noise coming from the front porch. She got up, opened the front door and looked out.

Wa-Yah stood staring at her with his big blue eyes.

"Wa-Yah! What are you doing here?" Janie asked. "I'm so glad to see you!"

Janie knelt down and threw her arms around his neck.

He was panting heavily and she wondered if he had run all the way from the river.

"I bet you would like to have something to eat," Janie said. "Just a minute, don't leave. I'll be right back."

Janie hurried to the kitchen got a handful of dog biscuits and a pan of water.

"Here you are," she said, putting the food and water down on the floor. "I put ice cubes in the water. I know you like them."

She sat down on the floor beside the wolf and watched while he ate the treats and drank the water. Janie laughed when he played with the ice cubes, rolling them around in the water.

When he finished eating and had his fill of cold water he left the porch and headed for the river He stopped once to look back to see if Janie was following him.

"Slow down," she called. "I'll come with you, but I'm having trouble keeping up"

He stopped and waited until she joined him before going on.

When they reached the water's edge Janie sat down.

"Wa-Yah! Come here!" she called.

When the wolf lay down beside her she stroked his head.

"I'm going to be gone for a while, Wa-Yah, but I'll

be back, so don't forget me."

She put her arms around his neck and hugged him close.

It was so peaceful sitting with her pet and thinking about the happy days ahead. The gurgling water and woodland noises made her sleepy after the big lunch, but she knew she didn't have time for a nap today. She looked up as a beautiful bluebird flew into the tree above her with a big bug in its feet and she heard the instant chirping of the baby chicks. She was surprised to see a white feather fall out of the nest and land at her feet. She knew this was a good omen. She picked up the feather and tucked it into her pocket as she stood.

"I must go now, old friend. I have a lot to do," she said, standing. "I'm getting married!"

CHAPTER FORTY-TWO

"How beautiful you look, Janie," Rose said, gazing at her granddaughter standing before her.

Janie wore a long turquoise-colored Tear Dress, trimmed in white designs. It was a traditional Cherokee dress and she had spent days making it to wear for her wedding.

Around her neck hung the turquoise stone necklace her Daddy had given her. She wore deer skin moccasins on her feet and a white feather in her hair.

"I like the feather," Rose said, stepping close to Janie and gently touching it.

"I'm wearing it in honor and remembrance of Great, Great Grandmother, White Feather," Janie smiled, "and for all the Cherokee women in our family who have come after her,"

"That's lovely," Rose said as tears gathered in her eyes.

"Where is the hiking stick?" Janie asked.

"Right here," Rose said, handing it to Janie.

Janie had attached a bouquet of Cherokee Roses to the top of it and she planned to carry the stick in her wedding.

Rose smiled at Janie while she wrapped a blue blanket around her granddaughter's shoulders. "This must be worn, you know, and Jim will wear one also. It represents the old lives and ways of you both."

Janie nodded.

"Now, are you ready to get married?"

"Yes," Janie said softly.

Rose adjusted the blanket around Janie's shoulders and stepped back to look at her granddaughter.

"Grandmother, listen. Do you hear the flute music?"

"Yes. It's so beautiful. He plays well, doesn't he?"

Janie nodded.

"The music means we need to go out on the deck, doesn't it?" Rose asked.

Janie nodded again.

They turned to leave the room and met Old Jess in the hall.

He was grinning from ear to ear.

"I like your ribbon shirt, Old Jess," Janie said. "It looks nice on you."

" Sgi (thank you). I am ready to begin," he said softly. "Do not come out until after I finish. I will do the smudging now and say a Cherokee prayer. When the music begins again come out on the deck."

He turned to leave and then turned back to face Janie. "You look beautiful," he said and then he was gone.

A short time later the flute music stopped.

"Grandmother, do you have everything? Janie whispered. "Do you have the corn?"

"Yes. Right here," Rose said, extending the basket filled with corn. "And here's the belt," she added, holding up a red and black finger-woven belt in her other hand.

After a few minutes Rose and Janie heard the flute music begin again.

"Time to go," Rose whispered, hugging Janie.

Janie pulled the blue blanket tightly around her shoulders and stepped out of the room.

"Oh," Janie asked nervously, turning to face her grandmother. "Who's got the wedding vase?"

"Janie," Rose said, "stop worrying. Everything's in place and ready."

"I'm sorry. Grandmother. I want my Cherokee wedding to be perfect."

"I know, honey," Rose responded, patting Janie's arm. "Tara and Millie have taken care of everything...and Hunter has helped."

Janie smiled.

The front deck of Rose's cabin was beautifully decorated. Pots holding large branches of colorful rhododendron and wild azalea blooms framed a backdrop for the ceremony. Grapevine streamers laced with spring wild flowers twined around the railing of the deck. Dark green Galax leaves held purple violets tied to each column and were topped with flat ivory candles along the railing.

The white folding chairs for the guests were lined up in rows, leaving an aisle down the center for the wedding party to use. Every chair was filled with family and friends.—all waiting to witness the happy occasion.

As Rose and Janie walked out on the deck and down the aisle Rose thought of another day long ago...the day when she and Lone Wolf had married in the same spot where her granddaughter would be standing today. How she wished her husband were here to stand beside her during the wedding. She felt his spirit and her heart skipped a beat like he had kissed her on the cheek.

A broad smile crossed Jim's face when he saw Janie coming down the aisle. There had been times when he thought this day would never come and he was so happy she would be his wife...his beloved.

He wore moccasins and the ribbon shirt she had made for him with a blue blanket draped around his shoulders.

Rose stood beside Janie, taking the place of Janie's deceased mother and Hunter stood beside Rose.

Jim's mother stood at his side, holding the traditional gift for exchange during the ceremony.

Old Jess began by praying for a long and happy life for the couple.

Then Janie gave Jim the belt she had made for him and watched while he tied it around his waist.

Rose stepped forward and gave Janie the basket of corn to exchange while Jim's mother gave him his gift of venison for Janie. After the exchange of the gifts Janie and Jim gave their gifts to Rose and Jim's mother to hold and they tied their blankets together pledging their mutual support within the marriage.

Old Jess held the wedding vase in front of them and Janie and Jim each took a sip of the corn drink from the double-sided wedding vase. Then they dropped the vase, breaking it to seal their wedding vows as they were now united as one. Later they would pick up the fragments of the vase and return them to Mother Earth.

"This is a Unity Blanket," Old Jess said, extending a white blanket toward Janie and Jim. He wrapped it around them to symbolize their union of marriage after the blue blankets were removed.

Without speaking Jim drew Janie into his arms quickly and kissed her, glowing with happiness.

They turned and faced Old Jess while he sang Amazing Grace in the Cherokee language. His voice was deep and resonant and the beautiful song echoed through the mountains

When he finished singing he turned to Jim and Janie and took their hands in his own.

"You now walk in one spirit," he said, smiling at the couple.

Jim pulled Janie into his arms again and kissed her while everyone in the audience stood and clapped their hands.

"Gv-ge-yu (I love you), my darling," Jim whispered to Janie.

"And Gv-ge-yu," Janie smiled, looking deep into Jim's eyes.

Over his shoulder Janie caught a glimpse of a rainbow in the western sky and knew that all was well in her life.

Epilogue

Two years later....

Janie sat on the cabin's porch enjoying the warm fall weather. The leaves were beginning to turn, dressing the trees for a colorful leaf season. She glanced up at the mountains in front of her.

"So much has happened during the past few years," she reminisced. "Jim escaped a terrible plane crash and we were married soon after he recovered. Hunter and Millie married and are expecting their first child. Steve has retired and he and Tara are often traveling, Emily and Brad have moved back to Kentucky and Wa-Yah...dear Wa-Yah...we found each other again," she added, looking at the wolf lying on the floor beside her. Janie reached over and stroked the top of his head, her touch waking him. He sat up, looked at her, then nuzzled her hand before lying back down.

Suddenly, in the silence of the afternoon, an animal's howl pierced the air.

Wa-Yah jumped up quickly and bounded down the steps running toward the river.

"Wa-Yah! Wa-Yah!" Janie called. "What's the matter?"

She ran to the edge of the porch, leaned on the railing and looked toward the river. She caught her breath when she saw the reason for Wa-Yah's quick departure.

Standing at the edge of the water was a mother wolf surrounded by three pups. When Wa-Yah reached them he nuzzled the grown wolf and then the babies

173

before they all disappeared into the woods together.

"Oh, Wa-Yah, you have a family now...and a mate for life," Janie said softly. "How wonderful!"

A whimper alerted Janie. She turned to look in the infant's bed and saw that her child had awakened.

Janie picked up the baby and cradled it in her arms. "What happiness you have brought to us." she whispered, then smiled, remembering the day of the baby's birth.

Jim had been very excited. When he came to Janie's hospital room after the baby arrived he was grinning from ear to ear.

"We have the most beautiful baby in the world," he raved. "I've seen her and I know this to be true!"

He leaned over and gave Janie a resounding smack on the lips.

"Did you know our baby has a birthmark?" he asked.

"What?"

"Our baby has a birthmark," he repeated.

Janie frowned, afraid that the birthmark might be unsightly. "Where is it?"

"On the lower part of her back...in the middle," Jim said, speaking rapidly.

"What does it look like?" Janie wanted to know.

"A little red arrowhead!"

"An arrowhead?"

"Yes, an arrowhead is on our little Cherokee's back," he smiled. "The nurse is bringing her in soon and then you can see it for yourself."

Janie remembered when the nurse brought the baby to the room she had slipped the diaper away and looked at the birthmark immediately. She had been pleased when she saw that it was in the shape of a beautiful tiny arrowhead Then, pushing the blanket aside, she had stroked the top of the little head, letting the infant's mass of black hair slip through her fingers.

Janie leaned down and kissed the infant's tiny cheek.

The baby moved in Janie's arms and brought her back to the present.

Looking down at the dark-haired infant, the new mother adjusted the pink blanket around her baby.

"My os-ti (little one)...my little Cherokee girl. You are so beautiful. I wish Grandmother Rose could have lived to see you...and Old Jess too. They would have loved you so much."

Janie reached over and picked up the hiking stick that was leaning against the porch railing nearby.

"Look at this," Janie said softly, holding the stick close to the baby's face. This beautiful hiking stick will belong to you someday. It's a symbol of the Cherokee women in our family. You must always care for it and protect it. You are a little Cherokee now, but one day you will be a grown woman. Be proud of your heritage, learn the history, the language, the culture of our people. Don't ever forget who you are ...especially the strength shown in our people's survival."

A slight breeze stirred around Janie and her baby, moving the infant's hair.

Janie smiled. She once more felt them again...the wings of the spirit of White Feather, her great, great grandmother.

While the baby's hair moved gently in the breeze the little one opened her eyes and smiled. She had felt it too.

Janie looked down at the baby and knew her little daughter, Angel Rose, was destined to carry on the legacy...the strength of Cherokee women.

About the Author

*N*ancy McIntosh was born and reared in Waycross, Georgia, After graduating from Georgia Southern University, she married her college sweetheart, Billy (Fuzz) Pafford, a teacher and high school coach, and moved to Lakeland, Georgia. They had two sons, Tim and Bryan. Tim lives in South Georgia.

After the deaths of her husband and son Bryan, Nancy retired from teaching school and moved to Cherokee, North Carolina, where she enjoys writing and substitute teaching in the Cherokee Indian School.

She is currently working on a new book, "School

Daze" (Sunshine and Shadows), about former students and their experiences while in her classroom.

Other Books by the Author:

WHITE FEATHER

CHEROKEE ROSE

(JANIE OF CHEROKEE is the third book in the "WHITE FEATHER" Trilogy)

OSCAR, THE LEGENDARY ALLIGATOR

For additional copies of this book, or if you are interested in receiving more information about how to acquire Nancy Pafford as a speaker for your school, club, dinner meeting or for a book signing, contact her at:

Nancy McIntosh Pafford
Post Office Box 528
Lakeland, Georgia 31635